AUREALIS
Australian Fantasy & Science Fiction

#100

Edited by
Dirk Strasser, Stephen Higgins and Michael Pryor

www.aurealis.com.au

CHIMAERA
PUBLICATIONS

CHIMAERA PUBLICATIONS
PO Box 2164, Mt Waverley, VIC 3149, Australia
editor@aurealis.com.au
www.aurealis.com.au

Aurealis #100
ISBN 978-1-922-03157-0
ISSN 1035-1205

PUBLISHERS: Dirk Strasser, Stephen Higgins, Michael Pryor and Volker Strasser

EDITORS: Dirk Strasser, Stephen Higgins and Michael Pryor

ASSOCIATE EDITORS: Scott Vandervalk and Terry Wood

LAYOUT and COVER ART: Andrew McKiernan

ART DIRECTOR: Lucy Strasser

WEBSITE MANAGER: James Firkins

SUBMISSIONS MANAGERS: Cas Le Nevez and Shel Sweeney

REVIEWS EDITOR: Deanne Sheldon-Collins

DIGITAL CONTENT COORDINATOR: Michael Pryor

EDITORIAL TEAM:
Julian Beath, Laura Birch, Taelor Carmichael, David Catt, Mark Fazackerley, Helen Fletcher, Brianna Flynn, Chris Foster, Emily Fox, Robert Goodman, Bronwyn Gregory, Janet Haigh, Steve Hocking, Jess Howard, Lachlan Huddy, Maree Kimberley, Paul Kotsabouikis, Michelle Kurrle, Cas Le Nevez, Aimée Lindorff, Sandra Makaresz, Emma Mann, Rebecca McEwen, Victoria McGlynn, Stephanie McLeay, Leah Milanovic, Harley Murphy, Alex Ness, Karen Parks, Megan Smith, James Spence, Shel Sweeney, Scott Vandervalk, Cassandra White, Terry Wood and Lea Z.

COVER ARTIST: Andrew J McKiernan
Andrew J McKiernan is a writer and illustrator from the Central Coast of New South Wales, and was Art Director for *Aurealis* for over 8 years. First published in 2007, his stories have since been short-listed for multiple Aurealis, Ditmar, and Australian Shadows awards, as well as being reprinted internationally and in a number of Year's Best anthologies. His short story collection, *Last Year, When We Were Young*, was awarded the 2014 AHWA Australian Shadows Award for Best Collected Work. 'The Message' was recently optioned to be produced as a short film by award-winning Australian director Tom Spark. www.andrewmckiernan.com

CHIMAERA LOGO by Gavin O'Keefe

Contents

Editorials

Fiction

Articles

From the Cloud
Dirk Strasser

Who would have thought on that fateful day in 1990 when Stephen Higgins and I decided to launch an Australian fantasy and science fiction magazine that we would still be here 27 years later publishing our hundredth issue? 1990 now seems another world away.

In 1990 Tim Berners-Lee published the first webpage, Nelson Mandela was released from prison, the official demolition of the Berlin Wall began, the hole in the ozone layer above the North Pole was discovered, and the first in-car GPS went on sale. It was the year when the top 50 movies included 6 science fiction and 6 fantasy movies such as Total Recall and Edward Scissorhands, the Sci/Fi Channel started transmitting on cable TV, the Hugo for Best Novel went to *Hyperion* by Dan Simmons, and the Ditmar for Best Australian Short Fiction went to Terry Dowling's 'The Quiet Redemption of Andy the House'.

It was also the year when *Aurealis #1* was published.

Homegrown science fiction and fantasy in Australia at the time wasn't exactly flourishing. Until we launched in September 1990, no Australian magazine that year had published any Australian SF professionally, and the major Australian publishers weren't publishing any SF novels. We decided to do something about it. But rather than launch the magazine with a lament about the parlous state of Australian SF, we decided instead to herald the Golden Age of Australian Science Fiction, a cry that Harlan Ellison picked up on a number of years later in Jack Dann's ground-breaking *Dreaming Down-Under* anthology.

As part of our plans for *Aurealis #100*, we decided to go back and contact everyone who appeared in *Aurealis #1* and ask them for a new story. The first story we ever accepted for *Aurealis* was David Tansey's 'And They Shall Wander All Their Days', a classy hard SF space travel story. David Tansey was at one point the author with the most *Aurealis* credits, but he has only recently come out of a twenty-year writing hiatus. Based on the quality of his clever, insightful and funny story 'The Cavity' in this issue, we're all hoping he finds the time to continue his return to science fiction. Michael Pryor's 'Talent' was the first story to appear in *Aurealis #1*. As most of you would be aware, Michael is now not only one of the co-editors and co-publishers of *Aurealis*, he is also one of Australia's most acclaimed SF authors and a much-loved writer of Young Adult and Children's books. His story in this issue, 'Shimmerflowers', is a powerful and dark tale of lost innocence.

Terry Dowling has also been going strong in the 27 years since his *Aurealis #1* story 'In the Dark Rush', and we've included his new story 'The Madlock Chair', a mind-blowingly original piece which creates a sense of the truly alien. Alex (formerly Sue) Isle's story 'Nightwings' appeared in our first issue, and his contribution to *Aurealis #100* is the zombie story 'All We Have Is Us' set in the most isolated capital city in the world. Geoffrey Maloney's contribution to *Aurealis #1* was '5 Cigarettes and 2 Snakes', and in this issue we are pleased to publish the funny, surprising and more than a little creepy pastiche of the Victorian sensational novel, 'The Bewitching of Dr Travidian'. Stephen Higgins ('Forest/Trees') and I ('The Mandelbrot Bet') have contributed stories of our own for the first time in many years. For various reasons, we were unable to contact the other three authors that appeared in our first issue: Dianne M Speter, Jai S Russell and George Turner. Since we now publish an overseas story in each issue, we have also included the poignant, magical (and appropriately named for our May issue) 'Mayfire' by Seattle-based science fiction and fantasy writer, Rebecca Birch.

Whereas issue #1 contained an interview by me with Australian SF's Grand Master, George Turner, issue #100 has an interview by CP Large with me about the history of *Aurealis*. Terry Wood also looks at the surprising possibilities of future technology in his article 'Robotics, AI and the Impending Techno-Apocalypse'. Book reviews only became a regular feature of *Aurealis* after the first issue, but *Aurealis #100* has our usual reviews of recently released SF/F titles. While our first issue featured the quirky and hard to categorise 'Science Fiction Hall of Fame', now we have the next instalment of the even quirkier and harder to categorise 'Secret History of Australia'.

The final words of our first editorial were 'Australian literature has never had a Golden Age of fantasy and science fiction. Perhaps it is shining just up ahead.' Little did we know when we wrote those hopeful, fateful words way back in 1990 that we would in 2017 be confirming that prophecy in our hundredth issue. We are now right in the middle of that Golden Age.

Thanks to those of you reading this, for joining us on the world-spanning ride to the future we've been on.

All the best from the Golden Age.

From the Cloud
Stephen Higgins

There have been a few milestones for *Aurealis* recently. We celebrated our 25th year not long ago, and now we've notched up 100 issues. The magazine has launched many careers and has provided an outlet for countless authors, editors, illustrators and reviewers. One aspect of the magazine that we often fail to remember is that it has also provided hours and hours of reading pleasure for thousands of people. Sometimes we get so caught up in the production of the magazine that we forget that it primarily exists to provide reading pleasure. I mean, I know that's what it does, but when I'm editing, and I hit that button that digitally launches a new issue, I'm relieved that I've got the issue out, and I don't give the end result of it too much thought. Anyway, this prompted me to go back and look at some of the issues we've published, and I'm pleased to say that I didn't really get to look at too many because I was so engrossed in a few of the stories. It was good to look over some old and some not so old stories just as an interested reader.

This brings me neatly to the point of quality control. We have a fantastic team of readers who go through all of the submissions and select the best. Then the three editors go through these and select the best of the best. We justify our individual decisions on these stories and every so often we end up with one editor having the deciding vote on a story. All of this ensures that our readers are getting the best possible stories. It means that *Aurealis* is held in high regard within the science fiction, fantasy and horror writing fraternities and it sets the bar high in terms of what is acceptable for our magazine. We are also very proud of our team of illustrators who adorn each story with fantastic art and who often do so under severe time constraints. The quality of the magazine is matched by the quality of the people who make it all happen, and who have made it happen over the years. Thank you all for your help in getting us to the 100 mark.

Finally, back to those who read the magazine. Hopefully this 100th issue will prompt some of you to go back and re-read some of the old issues. Maybe you even have some of those early 1990s ones that haven't been touched for ages. Drag them out and have a look. You'll be surprised at how well they stand up to another read. A special thanks to the many subscribers who have supported us over the years. Subscriptions are the lifeblood of an enterprise like this and I would like to take this opportunity to thank you for your past support and to encourage you to keep subscribing. You people help us to find the new bright names in science fiction, fantasy and horror, and I want to be able to read new stories by new authors as much as you do. And it is good to read some stories by some not so new authors as well. I'm referring to the fact that Dirk, Michael and I all have a story in this 100th edition. Way back in the early days of *Aurealis* we published stories by one or two of the editors every so often and none of us have had a story in the magazine for ages. I can't recall who had the idea of including stories by the editors but I will admit that I'm pleased and proud to have a story in the one hundredth issue of *Aurealis*.

From the Cloud
Michael Pryor

What have we learned from publishing one hundred issues of a science fiction/fantasy magazine in Australia?

Well, we've learned:

- That SF/fantasy readers are the best, most intelligent, most charismatic and most supportive readers on the planet.
- That lots of people want to write SF/fantasy. Lots and lots and lots of people.
- That sometimes it's hard to say exactly why a submitted story gets us excited, but we know it when we see it.
- That sometimes it's easy to say why a submitted story gets us excited. Observing the basic principles of good writing is an excellent start.
- That some people who submit stories to *Aurealis* really need to read more fantasy and/or science fiction.
- That watching the stellar trajectory of writers first featured in *Aurealis* gives us a warm inner glow.
- About the ups and downs of Australia Post.
- That conventions are amazing gatherings of like-minded people.
- That responding to changes in magazine layout, printing and distribution technology is important.
- That Australia has some extraordinarily talented writers and that all they need is a place to share their work.
- That Australia has some extraordinarily talented artists who love illustrating speculative fiction.
- That publishing a SF/fantasy magazine in Australia is a group effort and the result of the work of many, many dedicated people.
- And perseverance. We've learned a lot about perseverance.

Illustration by Andrew Saltmarsh

The Cavity

David Tansey

Wikipedia entry accessed 4 January 2030 [extracts]

The Cavity

From Wikipedia, the free encyclopaedia
Your donation will assist our work

The Cavity (also known as <u>van Bierlee's Vacuole</u>) is a spherical structure approximately 1200 kilometres across, about 600 kilometres below the surface of the Earth. It lies partly under the Southern Ocean and partly under the Australian mainland. It was discovered in 2028 by a team led by Dutch geophysicist <u>Boots van Bierlee</u> during seismic sounding of the continental shelf as part of a <u>manganese nodule</u> mining operation.

This anomalous area of the Earth's <u>mantle</u> is a perfect sphere. It shows on resonance imagery as an "empty space" [29], and is believed to be the only subterranean region at that depth that is not solid rock or magma. No other similar structure, of any size, has been found elsewhere in the mantle (although full examination of the sub-surface has not yet been conducted at the time of this entry, and the Cavity was found by accident). [30]

The Cavity is believed to have formed over four billion years ago when the Earth cooled and became a solid object. Various papers have been published presenting theories on how it was created [31] [32] [33]. One theory is that the Earth once enclosed a ball of ice, which then melted or evaporated, and that the source of this ice may have been a comet smashing into the liquid planet and then being covered by impact debris, which cooled and hardened.

The <u>volume</u> of the Cavity (using the formula $V = 4/3\,\pi\,r^3$) is estimated at 905 million cubic kilometres. The interior <u>surface area</u> of the Cavity (using the formula $V = 4\,\pi\,r^2$) is estimated at 4.5 million square kilometres, equal to the land areas of India and Argentina combined.

Diagram showing depth and size of The Cavity (not to scale):

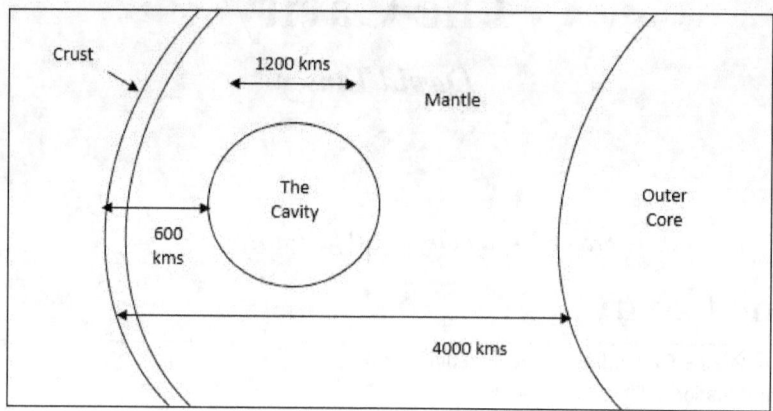

The relative small size of the Cavity compared with the total volume of the Earth means that it does not present a risk for the integrity of the planet's structure. "The worst thing that could happen," van Bierlee once joked, "is a big-ass <u>sinkhole</u> could open up under Australia. That would be no great loss." [citation needed]

In trying to visualise what the interior of the Cavity might look like, van Bierlee suggested that people watch the classic Hollywood movie *The Core*. There is a scene in the movie where the vehicle drilling towards the Earth's core comes across an empty space lined with giant crystals. Van Bierlee suggested imagining a space a thousand times larger, with its own climate and geography, and with a structural integrity that could not be broken just by its shell being pierced in one place. Just by van Bierlee referencing this movie, it is rumoured that almost a billion downloads of *The Core* subsequently took place, making more profit for the copyright owners than the movie did in its original release in 2003[34].

Early speculation [edit]

The discovery of the Cavity led to widespread discussion among followers of <u>Christianity</u> that it might be Hell, or at least be the inspiration for the concept of Hell being under the ground, a concept somehow conveyed to ancient man, then used as a basis for religious belief two thousand years ago. Others of that faith have argued that it might be Purgatory[35], halfway between Earth, and the path to Heaven once the penitent sinner has been purged of evil.

Other popular culture theories about the Cavity are that it is the location of the lost continent of <u>Atlantis</u>, or that it proves the <u>Hollow-Earth</u> theory. Another theory is that the place is a base for aliens who are studying humanity while keeping a low profile. Fans of the 20th century American horror author <u>H P Lovecraft</u> have proposed that it is the "sunken land of R'lyeh", home of the fearful god-like creature Cthulhu.

The quotation from van Bierlee above about the movie *The Core* has led people to believe she authorised the notion that the Cavity is full of "large crystals"[35]. Some have speculated that the Cavity could also contain "The Diamond as Big as the Ritz", a fictional mountain-sized <u>diamond</u> in a short story by American author <u>F Scott Fitzgerald</u>. Other would-be treasure hunters have described possible formations of <u>gold</u> as big as the Himalayas, dwarfing lakes of <u>platinum</u>. These dreams of subterranean riches ignore the fact that, if such volumes of precious gems or metals were ever discovered, they would no longer be rare, and so their commodity prices would plummet.

Internet businesses sprang up purporting to sell blocks of land on the interior surface of the Cavity. These offers usually involved a 5000-hectare plot (on the "gravity-down" side of the sphere, which forms only the lower third of it) for USD$5000, complete with a title deed, GPS co-ordinates and a cadastral map of where the plot is located. Another attractive reason for buying into the Cavity, according to these websites[36] [37], is that it is a <u>tax-free jurisdiction</u>.

Several entrepreneurs such as Ultimate Mancave and Down Under Estates are rumoured to have made hundreds of millions of dollars from this scheme (also see <u>scam</u>). Over 3.5 million plots were sold in the first three years, yielding over USD 17 billion dollars in total, before being shut down by corporate regulators. Unlike previous schemes to sell <u>plots of land on the Moon</u>, the entrepreneurs claim that this is not a scam, as the Cavity is within reach of humanity given the right level of technology, and they have as much right to issue title deeds as anyone else[38]. They claimed that, legally, no-one owns the Cavity, despite a partial claim on it by the Australian Government. Some international law experts have theorised that the Cavity is a <u>UN trust territory</u>, or if not, it should be if treaties could be amended before it is reached.

<u>Preppers</u> have stated that the Cavity should be explored and a vast shelter built for the best of humanity to take refuge, in case of meteor impact on the Earth, nuclear war, climate change or other catastrophic disaster.

Shortly before her suicide, when van Bierlee was asked by a reporter what she thought was inside the Cavity, she allegedly replied, "Yo mama." [39]

Wikipedia entry accessed 4 July 2040 [extracts]

The Cavity

From Wikipedia, the free encyclopaedia
A wholly-owned subsidary of NewsCorp

Since the discovery of the Cavity in 2028 extensive research by Earth-science specialists was conducted. The increase in technology for profiling sub-surface structures (itself driven by the discovery of the Cavity) has led to deeper and more accurate sensing and analysis of the sub-surface.

It has been confirmed [40] that the Cavity has a significantly lower pressure than the surrounding material and a much lower temperature; humans could survive inside the Cavity, or survive inside artificial habitats and/or with the assistance of environment suits. Technology being developed for human exploration of Mars and Venus has been deployed to ensure the survival of individuals in the Cavity.

The increased scrutiny of the Cavity and the use of better technology led to the breakthrough in 2039 by a <u>University of Shanghai</u> team finding that there were several "Spikes" radiating from the central sphere. The Cavity is now popularly referred to as "mace-shaped" after the head of the Middle Ages weapon, the <u>mace</u> (see diagram opposite). Each Spike is 400 to 500 kilometres long, 60 to 70 kilometres wide at its base, tapering to a "point" 2 to 3 kilometres across [41].

Like the main body of the Cavity, resonance feeds show that the Spikes are also hollow. One of the Spikes is angled in such a way that its "Tip" is only 92 kilometres below <u>Dyre's Island</u> in the eastern <u>Recherche Archipelago</u>. [Redirect from <u>Archipelago of the Recherche</u>] This is the closest point that any Tip comes to the Earth's surface. Dyre's Island is 78 kilometres off the uninhabited coast of Western Australia, and on the edge of the continental shelf. The island is ten hectares in size and home to several species of bird life, including albatross and penguins, and a seal colony of 300 animals.

The McQueen Expedition [edit]

The announcement of the mace-shaped nature of the Cavity inspired the McQueen Expedition to attempt to reach the Cavity, by piercing the Tip of the Spike that extends upwards towards Dyre's Island. The expedition was funded by a consortium including NewsCorp, the Amalgamated Universities of China and India, the Catholic Church, the Clinton Foundation, the Australian Government (Departments of External

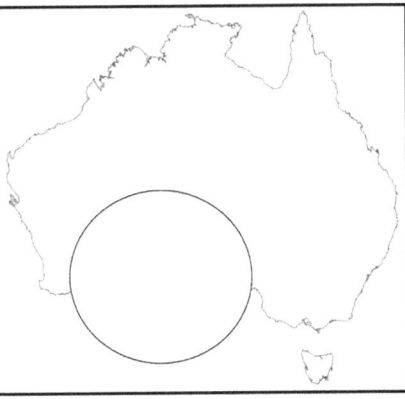

Territories and Foreign Affairs) and the Sicilian Investors' Trust [41].

The expedition cost has been estimated at 600 billion Australian dollars, and will take up to 20 years to accomplish[42].

The diagram above shows the relative location of the Cavity to Australia and the Southern Ocean (allowance must be made for the curvature of the Earth).

Although the Catholic Church was a joint venture partner in the expedition, the Pope warned that, if the Cavity is opened, the Devil will walk the Earth. This warning is based on an ancient codex held in the Vatican which reportedly contains a 17th Century Dutch map of Western Australia showing a "Way to the Pit" [43].

Some scientists have argued that, if the Cavity is breached, there is a risk that ancient bacteria or viruses could be released, possibly non-terrestrial in origin, which could wipe out humanity. Other more fanciful warnings are that cracking the Cavity could result in an outpouring of troglodytic zombies, or perhaps a plague that could turn humanity into the living dead [44].

It was also widely postulated that the Cavity might be a Dyson Sphere, that is, an artificial structure enclosing a dwarf star. This would mean that the interior surface had its own gravity and could provide a habitat of 4.5 million square kilometres, for an alien species or a group of engineered humans placed in quarantine by aliens[45]. This would require that the Cavity's interior has arable soil, rivers and lakes, and other environmental aspects which could support civilisation. The dwarf star would have been positioned by aliens, so that the hypothesised civilisation could have light and their crops could have a source of photosynthesis.

The <u>United Nations</u> voiced concern that, if the Cavity were found to contain an indigenous population, these people (or creatures) should be protected and not suffer the fate of indigenous populations under the colonialist invaders of the 16th to 20th centuries. It argued [46] that any people (including descendants of ancient man, Neanderthals or other species with a *Homo* prefix) found dwelling in the Cavity may automatically receive Australian citizenship, or alternatively may be covered by the <u>1951 Convention Relating to the Status of Refugees</u>.

The following diagram shows the intended path of the McQueen Expedition from Dyre's Island to the Cavity.

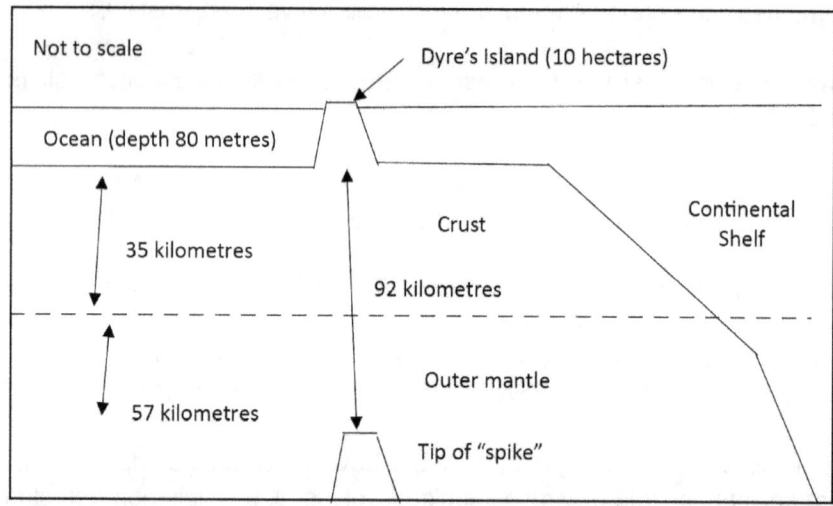

Immediately upon approval by the Australian Government and the United Nations (Dyre's Island lies in both a nature reserve and a UNESCO heritage protected area), Dyre's Island was transformed into the site of the world's deepest drilling operation.

The small surface area of the island was expanded using technical assistance from the Chinese government, based on the land reclamation technology they had used to grow <u>disputed islands</u> in the South China Sea.

A runway was built that could land Boeing 747s and Russian heavy-lift cargo transports. A deep port was carved into the side of the continental shelf at which vessels up to 50,000 tonnes with a draft of 10 metres could berth and be unloaded by dockside cranes. Cargo ships brought 100,000 ten-tonne concrete blocks which filled up the seabed around the island and supported all the structures built on the cement platform a hundred times the size of the original island. All bird nests and marine creatures had been humanely relocated to Mondrain Island by this time [47].

Fracking technology was used to blast a hole in the island and insert a supporting structure. At the bottom of the shaft an elevator was built using the "tube and hoist" technology that has long been used to rescue trapped miners, although on a much greater scale. This involves a cylindrical hole being bored into the bedrock, feeding sections of pipe into it, then lowering an "elevator car" into the pipe. Rather than just being able to haul up a miner, the new-tech elevator car could raise or lower a forty-foot container standing on its head.

It took over a year to dig the hole 10 kilometres deep. Once this was accomplished, the project team used their drilling equipment to create a small dome-shaped space from which they could plan the next phase: to penetrate the crust. Due to the mass of the Earth at that depth radio communications are not effective. The problem was solved by the laying of fibre-optic cable down the entire length of the shaft to each stage-gate, and from each node to the communications centre and then through wi-fi to each worker's protective suit.

Foreign interest [edit]

While these preparations were taking place, on the surface the many countries that then made up the world were staking claims on the Cavity.

The government of the United States of America claimed that the Cavity would make a uniquely protected base in case of nuclear war. They proposed that if the Cavity were found to be habitable, it could be the new location of the NORAD command base. The depth would ensure that it would remain intact after a theoretical nuclear war. As Australia was an ally of the USA, pressure was placed on the Australian Government under various military treaties to facilitate this, including from US President Chelsea Clinton [48].

The government of Israel proposed that the Cavity could be the location of the new <u>Palestinian homeland</u>. Various right-wing nationalist groups in Europe, Russia and elsewhere suggested that the growing numbers of asylum seekers and refugees pouring into their countries from the Middle East and Africa could be safely relocated there [49].

The Australian Government pointed out that legally they owned "the minerals under the land, all the way to the centre of the Earth", and also pointed out that half of the Cavity lay under Australia[50]. The other half lay under international waters, but the Cavity should be considered a contiguous space for legal purposes.

The Dutch Government claimed that, as one of their explorers had been the first European to discover the Recherche Archipelago in the 17th Century, *and* that a Dutch national had discovered the Cavity in the 21st Century, that they had proprietorial rights to any habitable land, minerals or other resources discovered in it[51].

Aboriginal Australian groups claimed <u>native title</u> to the area of the Cavity that lay under mainland Australia, the islands of the Recherche Archipelago and the adjacent seabed. Some claimed that the Cavity was the home of the <u>Rainbow Serpent</u>, who had created the <u>Dreamtime</u>, and that it should be left alone[52]. The courts in Australia were clogged with various claims, some vexatious and some bogged down for decades in legal grey zones. Specialist law firms made fortunes from the overlapping claims and disputes.

Various other countries, companies, associations and informal groups lodged "ownership" claims on the Cavity with the United Nations. These countries included those which had territorial claims on Antarctica, where it bounded the Southern Ocean: across a spectrum to countries that claimed they had pre-European trade with Aboriginal Australians, such as Indonesia, Malaysia, Vietnam, China and North Korea [citation needed].

Wikipedia entry accessed 3 March 2043 [extracts]

The Cavity

From Wikipedia, the free encyclopaedia
A wholly-owned subsidiary of NewsCorp (in liquidation)

The <u>Han Expedition</u> took over from the McQueen Expedition in 2042 to advance the digging operations from the surface world toward the Cavity.

At a depth of 10 kilometres, the carved-out area that was used to start the next phase of the operation, called the Dome, was a functional space 120 metres across and 20 metres high.

This phase used technology for tunnelling operations, such as drill heads 10 metres wide and vacuum systems for removing debris, orientated vertically instead of horizontally as they had been designed for. A shaft in the centre of the Dome's floor was commenced, and pipes made of <u>super-hard</u> materials were fed into the shaft as it was created (the super-hard material, developed in India by Tata Enterprises, had a hardness value of 300–400 gigapascals on the <u>Vickers hardness test</u>).

At the height of its activity the Dome held over three hundred workers[53]. Dormitories and support facilities were installed, modelled on those of <u>oil rigs</u>. The majority of workers were sourced from China, the <u>SAARC</u> countries, the Philippines and Indonesia, working in Australia on <u>section 457 visas</u>. Power, air and water were fed down the shaft from Dyre's Island to support the base for the next phase of excavation. Food, medical supplies and information/entertainment material were dropped in each container.

Each worker, when outside the habitat in the Dome, wore a full bodysuit which cooled them from the extremely high temperature and also carried oxygen tanks. The suits included helmets that could withstand the impact of a 10-kilogram rock falling 100 metres from above. The body of the suits was covered in <u>Kevlar</u>, apart from where the joints of the human body required mobility. The boots had one-inch thick pads that were resistant to any casual treading in magma. Overall, the suits could withstand 1000 degree temperatures centigrade, and extreme kg/square centimetre pressures.

Despite these protective coverings, the <u>worker loss rate</u> was an average of ten per month[54]. Wages paid to workers, and life insurance cover, were reportedly higher than in surface construction jobs, which made the wages paid by the expedition a good source of <u>foreign currency remittances</u> to the home countries of the workers. Many <u>unemployed Australian</u>s were offered jobs on the expedition, but only a handful took up the offer.

It took three years for the next phase to be completed. Drilling continued and the 35-kilometre deep crust was pierced by the super-hard tubing system. Dome 2.0 was constructed at the junction of the crust and the outer mantle, and was the same size and shape as the first Dome above it. Once the support base inside the Dome was finalised, excavation began ever deeper and downward.

On the surface, general interest in the Cavity was widespread. Reality TV shows purported to place a group of strangers in a simulated Cavity and subjected them to various hazards. Stand-up comedian Phil McCavity had sold-out shows in Las Vegas. Many dentists made clever advertisements for their practices based on supposedly making their patients' tooth cavities smaller than the Cavity. The political class in several countries formed Cavity policies, and some countries, such as Australia, established a Department of Cavity. In some countries such as in Uruguay, a Cavity political party was formed.

Wikipedia entry accessed 29 August 2050 [extracts]

The Cavity

From Wikipedia, the pay-by-view encyclopaedia
A division of the University of New South Wales

Another six years was required by the Han Expedition to drill downward through the mantle to the Tip of the Spike. This was reached in early 2049, followed by an operation to have Dome 3.0 hollowed out and a forward base constructed.

The Tip of the Spike was pierced on 1 January, 2050. The event was recorded in the live feed from expedition member Zhou Xia. The narrative of the event was fed up the fibre-optic cable to the surface base, and from there it was broadcast in near real time to a

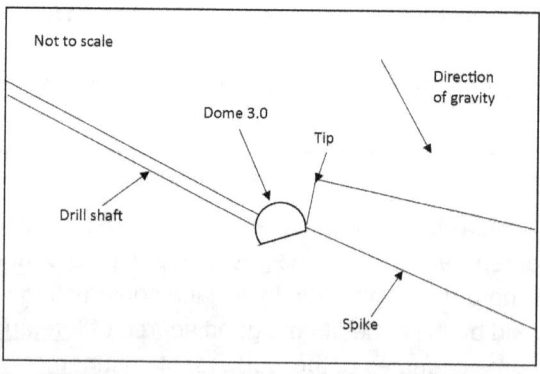

breathless and waiting world, similar, some say, to the live broadcast of the first moon landing in 1969. The text of this feed is reproduced below.

"We used the big drill to excavate the wall of the Dome where our scans had shown that the Spike pushed up against it. The outer shell of the Tip is over a hundred metres thick. When we knew we were close, the big drill was pulled back and a small team was sent in. C4 charges were used to break through the last section of wall into the Tip. We watched the charges blow from a safe distance, bringing down a curtain of grey rock and dust. When this grey curtain settled, a black hole now yawns.

"This is the first glimpse we have of the world below. We know this was only its extremity. I am fighting my feelings, trying to keep technical. The team move toward the opening. We pick our way across the ground. I happen to be the first one to reach the hole.

"My thoughts were very much on the <u>tactical nuke</u> which we've brought down to Dome 3.0. We cannot detonate it, but the controllers back on the surface can. If anything bad comes out of the Spike, they would turn the Dome to glass. Seal it forever. And us inside like insects in amber.

"Here I am, touching the hole. A faint wind is blowing out of it. I can't feel it under the weight of my suit, but someone has set up a pole with paper tapes stuck on it. Those tapes are flickering sideways.

"The rest of the team catch up with me. We walk into the hole made by the explosion. I take a step off the planet I know onto the floor of the Spike. Someone shines a super-bright torch beam ahead of us. Most of the team are carrying a piece of monitoring equipment, or a light, or something else useful. All of us have cameras built into the shoulder of our suits. I take a dozen steps further ahead. Someone collects an air sample in a jar.

"The Spike looks like a round tunnel. We know it is narrow at this end and wider where it opens into the Cavity 600 kilometres away. But we are like ants in a nest. It looks cylindrical from our perspective, because we are so small. We see that the floor of the Spike is covered with boulders from the size of footballs to houses, and every size and shape in-between. It is not traversable. The roof of the Spike has broken away in the direction of gravity, and the debris has ended up on the floor. There are no <u>stalagmites </u>or <u>stalactites</u>.

"We have a vehicle sitting in the Dome, a <u>tank</u> on caterpillar tracks with air-conned living quarters inside. We will not be able to use it here. The floor of the Spike is a jumble of rubble. Not good for a ground vehicle.

"Someone hand-launches a <u>drone</u> the size of a pigeon. The drone comes online and feeds us vision, to the little <u>HUD</u> inside the faceplate of our helmets. This means the vision also goes to the surface. The drone feed shows kilometre after kilometre of the same rubble. It reminds me a bit of the <u>Devil's Marbles</u> all stacked together. But endless. We will have to use the helicopter. I take a few steps further into the—"

[Transmission ceases as the roof of the blasted hole collapses, killing the entire forward team.]

Wikipedia entry accessed 29 August 2052 [extracts]

The Cavity

From Wikipedia, an accredited learning institution (CRICOS provider number 40300599ZZ) A division of the United Nations

Following the initial breach of the Spike and collapse of the blast hole, further work commenced after a suitable period of mourning. The hole between Dome 3.0 and the Tip was blasted open again. The remains of Zhou Xia and the other members of the forward team were not collectible[55], so the site was marked with a concrete <u>obelisk</u>.

As Zhou Xia had stated in her narrative, the Spike was not traversable using the "tank". Instead, the helicopter was used to progress the expedition. This <u>bespoke</u> craft was powered by two jet engines and four <u>graphite</u> rotors. The body of the craft could hold two pilots and six passengers. The cargo pod included food and water for several months, and scientific equipment and tents. <u>Line-of-sight</u> communication could be maintained from a dish atop the obelisk and a portable dish that could be set up on the highest points where the helicopter would alight from time to time.

The helicopter set off from Dome 3.0 on 15 January, 2050. It cruised at 100 kilometres per hour, which would mean a direct flight of six hours to reach the end of the Spike. However, the forward team stopped every 50 kilometres to take samples and make observations, which extended the trip time to two days. This included a camp-out on top of a massive flat-topped boulder.

The new forward team was led by Sadhika Chava (32-years-old, Indian national, female, a project management and navigation specialist). The other five team members, other than the pilots (who had combat experience), were duo-specialists in speleology/music, language/economics, botany/

astronomy, cryptozoology/architecture and poetry/survival science. The team composition was in line with best practice at that time[56] which saw multi-disciplinary teams of left/right brain duo-specialists.

The samples and readings the team took indicated that the rock debris on the floor of the Spike had similarities with <u>glacial moraine</u>; however, some material was rough and some smooth. Analysis showed that the rocks had the same composition as the surface of the Earth in terms of minerals, ores and precious metals. There was potential for mining, but with the location so hard-to-reach it would not be cost-effective.

There were puddles of water between the moraine that proved purer than anything on the surface. This water could be bottled and sent up to the surface, and marketed in a manner similar to <u>Fiji Water</u>, which until then could claim to be the purest aquifer water in the world. However, the going price for Cavity Water would need to be in the vicinity of $10,000 for a one-litre bottle for the enterprise to be profitable.

No sign of life was detected in the Spike. No bacteria, no moss, no insects, nor anything else. The forward team found that the air was breathable, with a similar composition to that on an unpolluted region of the surface. One expedition member described the taste of the air as: "alpine, with a hint of fjord, and an after-taste of wet dog" [57].

The engineers in Dome 3.0 constructed an airlock into the Spike. This consisted of a 40-foot container, with pressure-seal doors at each end, cemented into the hole. Inside was a decontamination chamber and changing rooms to swap out environment suits.

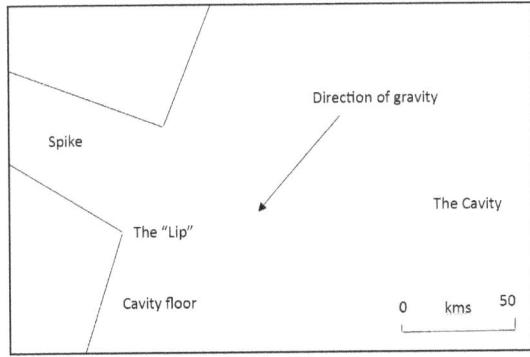

The team reached the "Lip" on 16 January, 2050, the place where the Spike grew of the body of the Cavity proper. It was fortunate that they had taken the helicopter, as the direction of gravity would not have permitted a ground vehicle to proceed (see diagram left).

The forward team set up a transmission dish on the edge of the Lip, so that line-of-sight communication could be maintained as they progressed into the body of the Cavity proper.

The temperature of the Cavity was in the range of 100° to 150° degrees centigrade, much cooler than the surrounding rock. This is explained by the "vacuole" nature of the structure; a contained sphere where the absence of solid matter itself affected temperature and pressure inside the overall structure of the mantle. The density of the material such as the rubble inside the Cavity was also much lighter than the surrounding rock.

This lighter temperature and pressure reduced the stress on the environmental suits, which were engineered to withstand a much harsher environment, allowing the team members greater freedom of movement to explore the place. Initial samples and measurements showed that the "floor" of the Cavity was composed of the same moraine-like material as that of the Spike. The helicopter made hops of 50 kilometres, and at each stop samples were taken and analysed, with the results sent back up the comms line.

On 20 January, Chava reported: "Three days in. The properties of the Cavity look the same as the Spike down which we got here. A lot of rubble on the floor—some big, some medium, some pebbles. Rubble and pebbles—hey, they should film the next Flintstones movie here. Water and air chemistry are constant. Though we've only just crossed the Lip, my greatest worry is that we're going to die of boredom. Nothing happens here" [58].

Wikipedia entry accessed 22 May 2053 [extracts]

The Cavity

From Wikipedia, the pay-by-view encyclopaedia
A subsidiary of the WikiLeaks Corporation

Over the years 2051 to 2053 the Han Expedition continued its laborious exploration of the Cavity proper.

During this period, the popularity of the expedition's work increased around the world, resulting in what some sociologists have called "obsession", bordering on "mass hypnosis" or "mass hysteria". Numerous social media sites sprang up devoted to discussion of what might lie within the Cavity, who or what created it, and to what purpose it might be put, based on the evidence being sent up the pipeline.

Millions of people enrolled in geoscience courses, although the completion rate of courses was low as much of this was based on devotion, bordered on what could be called a new religion. Groups formed (independently and in diverse locations) which came together as congregations to study, philosophise and/or worship the Cavity. The most prominent of these was the New Temple of Cavitarians. At its height the New Temple boasted over a hundred million members[59], mostly in Latin American and Asian countries.

In the United States, when author Jeff Long, who had written novels about a subterranean civilisation called the Hadals, passed away of natural causes, the funeral home in New York where he reposed was mobbed and his body torn apart by Cavitarians seeking saintly relics.

Some psychologists theorised that the Cavity may be a Freudian metaphor for the uterus. It was a place deep and safe in the body of the Earth, with a narrow tube to the external world. It offered concepts of birth and rebirth, renewal, a nutrient-rich environment, safety, warmth and love. Other psychologists compared the Cavity to other body parts, including the cranium, the bladder and even the rectum[60].

Others, such as conspiracy theorist David Icke, claimed that the Cavity did not exist at all, that it was a distraction created by the United Nations, the Illuminati or some other secret society, to take peoples' minds off deteriorating living standards, the growth of war, famine, rampant crime, economic collapse and other more mundane issues[61].

The worker gangs who maintained the surface base on Dyre's Island, plus the various infrastructure from Dome 1.0 to Dome 3.0, were infiltrated by religious fanatics who stowed away on cargo shipments heading down the super-hard tube. It was rumoured that one stowaway, a male native of Algeria, made it as far as the Spike with a bomb before being detected, although no further word was heard about this person or what happened to him.

The Intergovernmental Panel on Climate Change (IPCC) claimed that the Cavity was the reason why no global warming had been detected since the late 1990s. It had been thought that the world's ocean deeps were acting as a heat trap; the Cavity provided an alternative suspect. Climate change sceptic <u>Lord Monckton</u> proposed that a permanent tube should be opened from the surface into the coolness of the Cavity, which would suck in the theoretically heated air of the Earth's atmosphere and reverse any "imaginary climate change" [62].

The Russian government announced that it had developed a <u>daisy cutter</u> warhead which could penetrate the 600 kilometres of solid rock between the Earth's surface and the Cavity, in the event that NORAD relocated there. The alleged weapon was a satellite-based structure nicknamed the <u>Death Star</u>. This claim was generally ridiculed as puffery on the part of Russia's new ultra-nationalist president; although, as a precaution, the US government announced that it was working on sub-surface nuclear weapon-based missile defences that could counteract such a threat, nicknamed <u>Hell-Boy</u>.

Peace activists argued that there was a risk that a collision between the Death Star's daisy cutter and the Hell-Boy counter-measure may "blow up the whole fucking planet like a king-hit on a piñata" [63].

Wikipedia entry accessed 22 October 2056 [extracts]

The Cavity

From Wikipedia, an open source of the Voice of Freedom
Please make donations directly to our Tehran headquarters

In 2054 the exploration of the Cavity continued. The forward team was swapped out every six weeks to avoid fatigue, and to expose more people to the frontier. Expedition members who did their stint and returned to the surface were often photographed in tops saying: "I went to the Cavity and all they gave me was this lousy t-shirt" [64].

As the Cavity's structure unfolded under the forward team, pictures of the same monotonous geoscape was transmitted back to the surface. Drone footage showed that the roof had fallen away in the distant past, and the debris lay smashed on the floor (in the direction of gravity). The roof was undulating, but not jagged. The floor had lain undisturbed for billions of years. Water puddles here and there were pure and lifeless. There was little erosion from flowing water. No endemic life was found; that is, the Cavity contained no life apart from the expedition members and whatever bugs they in advertently carried in from the surface. Importantly, no <u>fossils</u> were discovered.

Three hundred kilometres beyond the Lip, a new base was constructed on a large flat boulder to progress the exploration. This was nicknamed "the Castle" [65]. Its outer wall was made of used cargo containers, with a roof marked out into four helipads. Inside was home to eighty support crew. Several more helicopters were brought down from the surface to the Castle to increase the rate of exploration.

Other drones sent ahead of the lead helicopter showed the same landscape curving around the lower third of the Cavity, seemingly forever. The boring footage led to questions being asked about the purpose of the expedition, as well as its cost (by then estimated at four trillion US dollars). The new project manager, AK Yuen, attempted to spin the geologically interesting features of the Cavity, while emphasising that only two percent of its area had so far been explored. She is famous for proclaiming: "The big find is yet to come!" [66].

The lack of anything interesting—no subsurface civilisation, no devil, zombies or Cthulhu, no mountains of gold or diamonds as big as the Ritz—led to conspiracy theories that there was an official cover-up of whatever actually existed inside the Cavity. This sent the religious fanatics, social media trolls and the general population into a frenzy overdrive, which led to political repercussions and social engineering impacts.

A group known as Cavity-Sceptics broadcast messages insisting that the McQueen and Han Expeditions had been invented, much in the same way that the 1969 moon landing was alleged to be faked, or at best that they were a form of reality TV. There were claims that the footage from the Spike sent back to the surface was actually filmed inside the lava tubes of Queensland.

Some urged that not only were the expeditions faked, but the Cavity did not exist at all. It had been a plot to distract humanity, or give people hope, a sense of wonder, or a scheme to escalate military spending. It was said to be a belief system to replace climate change, now that the planet was proved to be cooling, and in fact facing a new Little Ice Age[67].

Another group of bloggers insisted that the Cavity and the expeditions sent into it were real, but that what they discovered had been covered up because it was something that humanity could not handle. The most common theory was that the Cavity contained a habitable world with fertile soil, forests and vegetation, and possibly an advanced civilisation that wanted to share its technology with humanity. Certain groups[68] were alleged to be negotiating with the <u>Native Cavitians</u> to obtain this technology, while the majority of humanity would miss out. These special groups, such as the <u>Trump Foundation</u>, would allegedly become incredibly rich and powerful, while the rest of humanity lingered in poverty and ignorance.

As a reaction to these negative media reports, the expedition started to include ordinary members of society on the drops through the crust and mantle, and on board the helicopter sorties. These people were selected in a lottery and were intended to be independent observers, with their testimony proving that the expeditions were real. Later, journalists, officials of <u>NGOs</u> and even members of the Cavity-Sceptics organisations were brought down to Dome 3.0 and into the Spike to provide testimony as to the veracity of the venture.

Some visitors were even taken into the Cavity proper, where their helicopter transport landed on a boulder and powered down. All lights were turned off, so the visitors could experience the "intense blackness" of the 1200 kilometre void. This trick had been used for centuries by guides in cave systems to demonstrate the complete lack of light. Night vision goggles and similar technology were useless in such a place. After experiencing the complete blackness for three minutes, many visitors came away with feelings variously described as "nausea", "giddiness", "falling into the sky" and "revelation" [69] [70].

Some Cavity-Sceptics claimed that the visitors had not actually been to the Cavity (which did not exist), but had been variously hypnotised, paid off or tricked into believing that that they were in the Cavity when they were actually inside the <u>Jenolan Caves</u>.

Another tactic of the project manager to give credibility to the Cavity was to change the mission parameters. Large drones were sent off in all directions to explore the vast emptiness, while the forward team concentrated on reaching the most visible landmark within reach of the Castle, being the opening of the next nearest Spike.

Spike 2 was only 500 kilometres from the Castle. It descended vertically, well-like, in the direction of gravity. The forward team headed directly for it in the helicopter, without pausing to take readings. It was hoped that Spike 2 would present something different from what had already been discovered. The Lip of Spike 2 was reached in a few hours. It proved to be an opening 65 kilometres across, completely clogged with boulders. This prevented the helicopter from entering Spike 2, but small drones were able to flit between them. Readings showed that its tip, 555 kilometres below, was incredibly hot, possibly molten, and the heat and pressure would destroy helicopters and suited team members.

Aware of the failing ratings of interest in the Cavity, the forward team was then ordered, in January 2056, toward Spike 3, 650 kilometres away from Spike 2. It flew directly there.

Spike 3 was different from Spike 2, in that it lay almost perfectly horizontal to the direction of gravity, so it had a floor. The helicopter hovered in its mouth, training its floodlights into Spike 3. The floor was covered with boulders of every shape and size, puddles of water, and not much else. It looked identical to a slice of the floor of the Cavity proper.

Despite the routine and unchanging scientific reports sent back to the surface, those outlets devoted to the Cavity showed higher than ever ratings. Millions of people reported on social media that they dreamed of the Cavity every night. Uncountable TV shows, blogs, tweets, bleats and boggs were devoted to seemingly endless discussion of the Cavity. The less that real information was provided to the Cavity-verse, the more speculation and fantasy grew. The memes were on the theme of: "Why was the Cavity so boring? What did it really hide? Was the real nature of it being concealed and, if so, by who?" [71].

Wikipedia entry accessed 12 April 2061 [extracts]

The Cavity

From Wikipedia, an Information Unit of the USE
Final entry on last day of the Internet's operation

Copy and pasted text of speech of President of the United States of Earth (USE), Georgina Galloway, on 12 April, 2061.

"My fellow human beings,

"I stand before you today with a heavy heart. I need to tell you that, two days ago, contact was lost with the forward team exploring the Cavity. A day ago, we lost contact with Dome 3.0, and as of this morning we have not heard from Dome 2.0. I have ordered the surface base on Dyre's Island to be evacuated, and for the Australian forces to surround the island with warships and aircraft so that no-one else can go down there.

"No effort will be made to rescue those expedition members and visitors spread across the Cavity. They will have to make their own way out.

"These precautions see the end of decades of exploration. The Cavity has proven not to hold any natural resources which could be exploited to assist us on the surface. There is no race of new people that we could make friends with. There's no spectacular subterranean structures that we could marvel at. It's just a blank space—one might call it… a cavity.

"The expedition to explore the Cavity over the last four decades has consumed several trillion dollars. More importantly, it has had the world focused on something under our feet, about which we were theorising, dreaming, inventing new belief systems, and generally wasting time on social media. We, all nine billion of us, were like the teenager with his or her head down on a personal communication device, ignorant to the fact that we were walking past a burning house.

"The money has run out. All of it. We can't afford to rescue the last of the explorers down there. The world is bankrupt. There are widespread extreme shortages of food, water and energy. Local wars have broken out on all continents, including Antarctica.

"This speech will be broadcast on all media channels. It may be the last broadcast of the USE Government. I am informed that the servers which support the Internet will fail soon.

"Please stay in your homes. Learn from this experience. Try to become self-sufficient. Consider pragmatism over dreams. Prepare to defend yourself against the dangers that are closer than you think.

"Goodbye, and may the Belief Being have mercy on your channels."

Disambiguation [edit]

The Author: David Tansey

David Tansey was the first person to have a story accepted by *Aurealis*, and had four stories in the first six issues. He was active in the genre in the late 80s and early 90s, then suspended writing for 20 years. David is a freelance consultant based in Canberra who advises governments on their tax policy and administration. He has worked in several countries including Fiji (staying there seven years, including during the last two coups), Nepal, Mongolia and Romania. He has masters' degrees in tax and management.

Story Behind the Story

In 2015, after 20 years of not putting pen to paper, I had a dream about 'The Cavity' as described in the story. I felt compelled to write it down and explore what would be the impact of such a discovery, overlain with my observations of today's society. There is humour in there, but it was not intentional. The idea of using Wikipedia as the framework for the story came when I was researching the Earth's structure. There was an intention to be a bit preachy about the way the world uses social media and believe in just about anything.

The Illustrator: Andrew Saltmarsh

Born and raised in country South Australia, Andrew now resides in Melbourne where he works in an office by day and illustrates by night. You can follow his work at facebook.com/saltysart.

Illustration by Kim Lennard

Shimmerflowers

Michael Pryor

The shimmerflowers were my idea. It took me ages but I found some up on the crag. Old Marda said that shimmerflowers were killing us because they used water that should have gone to our crops but she says everything is killing us so what's the difference? Anyway Juleen looked pretty in her Vigil gown barefoot and holding the bunch of soft and white and puffy shimmerflowers on the rock in square in the middle of town waiting for her companion.

In eight years' time when I'm sixteen when the Father Moon is in the sky alongside the Daughter Moon and it's my Vigil Day I'll climb the ladder to the top of the rock pick up the stone crown put it on my head and wait for my companion to come. Please please please let it be a star mason. Or a rolypoly. Or something else good.

Our village is tiny so we don't have many people turning sixteen which means we don't have many Vigil Days. The last person to have one was Braga and he got a razor lizard. Most people went 'Ew!' which was mean. I thought the razor lizard was cute with its claws and curly tail and wobbly eyes. It rides on Braga's shoulder when he's tilling the fields and it catches flies and keeps them away from Braga's face. That's a good companion.

Old Marda said the razor lizard would kill Braga but Old Marda is crazy. Companions help people not kill them. They help us and they keep our grown-up souls safe I hope Juleen gets a nice companion. A fumblelark, maybe. A companion that sings would be fun.

The village Vigil Book says there are four companions that sing. The fumblelark and the glassine and the whistler and the tremash. All of them except the tremash look like birds but the picture of the tremash makes it look like a big caterpillar.

We've never had a tremash in our village.

I gave Juleen her flowers just after dawn when her Vigil truly began. I had to stand on tiptoes and stretch. She held them to her face and rubbed her cheeks against the spongey softness of the petals even though shimmerflowers don't have much smell. Her long black hair draped around her face and her stone crown nearly slipped off when she took a big breath. 'Oh, Panny, my favourites! Thank you!'

'Don't let the crown fall or it'll turn to sand and we'll have to make another.'

She reached up and steadied it. 'I know, Panny.'

'That's what the Vigil Book says.'

She smiled like the sun. 'It does, little brother and if anyone would know, you would.'

'Nothing yet?'

She laughed. 'You would have heard me if I'd been lucky enough for an early arrival.'

'Braga had to wait all day and into the night before his companion came.'

'I know. And I know the story of Wilga the Clumsy.'

Everyone knew the story of Wilga the Clumsy and how her stone crown fell off and she tripped on it and fell off the rock and was companionless forever after until her soul dwindled and she died. I don't know if I believe it though. Our rock is only a few paces across but how could anyone fall off? Even if nature calls you'd have to be really silly to fall. The facility on the north of the rock is solid as it hangs out over the edge. Smelly but solid.

The Vigil was grand and wonderful and all that but it had to have a smelly side. People are people, after all, even on their Vigil Day.

The top of the rock is flat and bare. If the weather is bad and if it's the wrong time of year, the Vigil can be a long, long day. Everyone still looks forward to it, though, no matter what time of the year their Vigil Day falls on because a companion can make all the difference.

Times are hard after all. The earth is thin these days. Plants struggle. Our flocks, our goats and our sheep, are skinny. If you believe the oldsters—and I don't, as they're awful liars—we used to have good years every now and then. Not anymore. We used to even trade with other villagers, they say, but not anymore. Last year Braga walked a whole day to where they said the nearest village was but when he came back he said there was nothing there.

Life is hard but companions help. Companions keep your soul safe. They don't eat, don't drink and they're an extra pair of eyes. They can do simple tasks. They can watch and report. The big ones can keep you warm. Everyone wants a clever and muscular companion but even a razor lizard can be useful. I like to look at all the companions in the Vigil Book and wonder which one I'll get. When I was little, Juleen read it to me until I learned the words. She made up funny stories about the companions and I used to laugh a lot.

The sun rose. People started to come out of their houses on their way to the fields or their workshops. Nearly all of them came to the rock and wished Juleen luck. Ma and Da stood around for a while and told her the best way to sit on top of the rock. Juleen listened carefully, nodding even though she had heard the same advice every night for the past month. I nearly laughed when Da told her, *again*, to tie her hair back just in case the wind came up and blew it in her face and made her trip and fall off the rock.

I had already fed the pigs and swept out the boot room so my morning chores were all done. Da tried to find some more for me but Ma turned him around and herded him away from the rock. She didn't want him making Juleen nervous.

The sky was lightening and it was now a soft, pale blue. Juleen was sitting cross-legged and leaning over the edge. She straightened her stone crown and then drummed her fingers on her knees.

'Braga said he got an itch on the back of his neck just before his companion arrived,' I called up to her.

'Braga is always scratching himself, Panny. It doesn't mean anything special.' She looked towards the fields. 'You sound as if you've been talking to Braga a lot.'

'He got mad at all the questions.'

'I'm sure he did.'

'It didn't matter. I wanted answers to stuff that isn't in the Vigil Book and I asked him 'til I got them.'

'All that reading. You probably know more about the Vigil than I do.'

'I even talked to Old Marda.'

'You did? What did—'

Juleen blinked. She looked left then right, slowly, as if she heard her name being called but wasn't sure from which direction the call came. She put her flowers down and stood. She held her arms away from her sides and wiggled her fingers.

'Juleen?'

'Shh.'

She moved to the middle of the rock and she turned in a circle, very, very slowly. She looked up at the sky. I wanted to call out to her but I wasn't sure she'd hear.

A monster appeared on top of the rock right in front of Juleen and I screamed. It was twice as tall as a tall man and much, much broader. It was mostly head, with spindly arms and legs, scaly and warty as a marsh pig with eyes like moons and it was so horrible that I screamed again.

Juleen screamed too as the monster rounded on her. It was so big that it took up most of the room on top of the rock and when it moved it knocked her aside so she teetered on the edge. She didn't scream this time but I did as she swung her arms and flapped for balance half there but half not and half about to fall off the rock.

She lost and she fell.

With a hiss the monster shot out one skinny arm. It grew. Longer and longer it stretched until it grabbed Juleen by the shoulder and wrenched her back from the edge. The monster dragged her close and used both hands to hold her up so she dangled by her shoulders. Then its awful mouth opened tall and wide as a barn door.

The monster swallowed my sister whole, danced a little jig on top of the rock, spat out the stone crown, and disappeared.

* * *

The whole village came galloping at all the screaming but nobody believed me nobody but Old Marda and nobody listened to her anyway They all thought that Juleen had run away, even Ma and Da, even though Juleen had no reason to. Everyone liked her. She was happy. She was smart. She couldn't wait for her Vigil Day to come so she could get a companion and be an adult and have her soul safe.

And now she was gone. People talked, cried and went looking for her and sent their companions out too but the search didn't last long. Too much to do in the village.

I missed my sister. I cried for weeks, just like Ma and Da, and even though that faded the hurt stayed behind. She looked so pretty so good so happy and a monster ate her on her special day. It wasn't fair and I had to carry the hurt with me as well as the worry.

I was the next oldest in the village so my Vigil Day was next and for the first time I was scared. Even though the Vigil Book didn't say anything about monsters one came for Juleen and one could be waiting for me.

Ma and Da argued a lot after Juleen was taken. Ma blamed Da. Da blamed Ma. Their companions even bickered, growlbear and patchy, rumbling and clicking. Ma and Da blamed me sometimes but I knew they didn't really mean it. They were just looking for a reason and they didn't like it when I told them that a monster was the reason. After a while people started looking at me the same way they looked at Old Marda so I stopped telling them about the monster with its spindly arms and giant mouth and the way it danced a jig before it vanished.

Every day after I did my morning chores I went to the rock and walked around it slowly even past the stinky part until my neck grew sore from looking up. Whenever I could I got the Vigil Book and turned the pages looking for answers but I couldn't find any.

What would happen when my Vigil Day came?

* * *

I was there when Juleen came back. One year to the day she came back. And she came back with a companion.

I'd gone to the rock early hoping but not really thinking something might happen. I walked around the rock as usual looking up as usual. Then she was there and I gave a shout that was half surprise and half hurt.

She was wearing the same white gown and her feet were streaked with yellow clay. Her arms were wrapped tightly around herself as if she were cold. She looked down at me and a smile crept onto her face. It was sly and mean and it wasn't a Juleen smile at all.

My hands flew up like frightened birds. 'Juleen!' I screamed. 'Juleen!

Her grin widened. She bared her teeth. Then people started coming out of their houses at all the noise. Juleen glanced at them nodded at me closed her eyes and lay down until she was stretched out on top of the rock.

I waved wildly. 'It's Juleen! She's back!'

Braga fetched the ladder. With a face like thunder gone wrong Da climbed the ladder picked up his long lost daughter cradled her to his chest with one arm and brought her down.

Ma was crying and she wasn't the only one. All the oldsters in the village were crying and their companions were leaking tears too. Everyone else was smiling and slapping backs. Companions scampered and flapped and wriggled. I clasped my hands together so tightly they hurt.

Juleen opened her eyes and everyone cheered.

Da settled her on her feet but he kept an arm around her shoulders. She swayed a little and her head bobbed as if she were very very tired. She lifted her chin lowered her arms and the crowd hushed.

Juleen had a companion in her hands. It was like a great furry spider but with four legs instead of eight. They moved in a way that made my stomach turn as if they didn't have joints or even bones. It had a face with wide round eyes and a wide round mouth. It stood on its hind legs and bent towards us then leaned left and leaned right while Juleen smiled at it. She stroked it with a hand and it settled. 'I'm so glad to be back,' she said and she burst into tears.

'It's not in the book,' I said. 'What is it?' I asked but my question was lost in the cheers. Braga stomped his feet and bellowed like a bull while his razor lizard hooted happily. Da let Ma take his place and she hugged Juleen as if she was going to squeeze the life out of her. Da leaned against the rock and wiped his face with the back of his hand again and again and his growlbear bumbled around and tried to trip him over.

Everyone was chattering, laughing, grinning and using words like 'miracle' and 'blessing' and our flint hard lives were sunny for a while.

Old Marda, though, took one look at Juleen and her spindly companion and she backed away as if a rabid dog had wandered into town and she didn't want to draw its attention. She covered her face with her shawl and shuffled off to where her hut was hidden out past the end of town in the middle of the few trees we had left.

Feasts are never declared in our village. They just happen and this one did and rolled on into the night. People brought food. They brought jugs of cider. They brought hallowberry wine. The day was fine so tables and chairs were brought out into the square. Juleen sat in our best chair. Braga brought his drum and Da dragged out his fiddle. Ma made a speech but no-one could understand most of it because of her sobbing. We clapped anyway.

Juleen sat there looking dazed and pretty with her strange companion on her shoulder. No she couldn't remember a thing not one thing from her whole Day or the year after until she woke up in her father's arms. Was there a monster? She couldn't say. Where has she been? She didn't know. How did she feel? Glad to be home.

I didn't get to ask her anything. She turned away from me whenever I approached. She tugged at forearms and asked people about what had happened while she'd been away and wouldn't talk to me.

I wasn't hungry but Da made me take one of his cheese pastries. I held it in my hand and slipped through the crowd and climbed up to the top of the old town house where I could watch them adoring my sister.

'You're not happy, Panny.'

Old Marda had a large tankard of cider, and a large cup of hallowberry wine next to where she sat with her back against the crumbledown chimney. Her stone sparrow companion was pecking at a crust of bread. Old Marda had crumbs and gravy stains down her front but they were easy to miss. Old Marda was never picky when it came to cleanliness.

'Of course I am,' I said. 'My sister is back.'

Old Marda tilted her head and squinted at my sister in the middle of the lantern light. 'Is she?'

I pointed.

'Huh,' Old Marda said. 'What do you think of that companion of hers?'

'What is it?'

'No idea.'

'It's not in the book.'

'Lots of things aren't in the book.'

'Really?'

'Really. I'd keep an eye on it if I were you.'

'What? Do you think it's going to kill us?'

'Everything's trying to kill us, Panny, why should it be any different?' She poked a finger at me. 'You going to eat that pastry?'

* * *

Juleen fitted back into our village as if she had never been gone. She took charge of the fishpond and everyone was glad because Old Marda and her stone sparrow had been taking care of it and they knew nothing about the care of fish. The eels were skinny and tasted of mud under her stewardship. When Juleen took over, her companion scurried around the fishpond clearing away loose weed and scraping scum from the reeds. It was good at gutting fish, too, for it had claws that would shoot out of its furry limbs when needed. Slit, snip, grope, and drag all done in an instant. With its help Juleen made everything right and the fish were fat and juicy again.

She never wore shoes. No matter the weather she was always barefoot. People forgave her this little strangeness though. Juleen was back, wasn't she?

People didn't talk about Juleen and Braga though. Before Juleen was taken, talk was about that these two young folk would be right together. It wasn't Juleen's absence, though, that put a stop to the talk. It was Braga. His razor lizard disappeared. That never happens. People's companions sometimes die but their person dies soon after because their soul isn't safe anymore and that's that. A companion doesn't just go missing while their person panics and stomps around all over the place looking for it. Braga said that he woke up and it was gone. I heard some of the old folk muttering saying that Braga must have killed it by accident and didn't want to tell anyone.

That day I saw Juleen at the fishpond hiding from the sun and giggling into her companion's ear while it shivered and shook.

Once his razor lizard disappeared Braga was broken. He was worse than Old Marda. He couldn't be trusted to till in the fields anymore because he hacked away at crops as well as weeds. He talked to himself all the time. Loud and rambling and making no sense or quiet muttering that made me feel sorry for him even though it was scary. He wouldn't look anyone in the eye, either. His gaze was wild and flitted from side to side and up and down looking for his lost companion all the time.

Parents kept their children away from him.

Juleen had always been nice to me and she was nice to me now. She kept the choicest fish for me. She praised me on the way I fed the pigs. She told Ma and Da that she was lucky to have a sister like me. She even let me pat her companion and I did once but it gave me the shivers and I didn't like the way it cocked its little head at me so I never did again.

Juleen did all this but she didn't do it with her heart. It was a pretend game she played when everyone was looking. I knew because I watched her and I saw her face when she thought she was by herself. The mean smile lived on her face, the smile bobby cats have when they find a wall mouse to play with. She would sit for hours whispering in the ear of her spindly companion or having it whisper into her ears, her hands in her lap and teeth bared, thinking thoughts that Juleen would never have thought.

* * *

Other companions disappeared. Widow Phyla's faith frog. The friendly rock marten that belonged to Mollon the smith. Sesta's companion went too. She was the woman who made the ladder that Juleen used to climb the rock for her Vigil and her companion was a great big scowser with a black and white pelt. It spent most of its time snoozing on her doormat until it went, just like that.

All of them vanished while their people slept and they were never the same again. Sesta left the village without a word and marched in the direction of the setting sun with no food and no water and the oldsters shook their heads but didn't try to stop her. She didn't come back.

Juleen was as upset as anyone. She sent her companion searching and she combed the village like the rest of us. No-one but me saw her mean smile later after all the searchers had given up and I spied on her and her companion near the fishpond.

The year was turning, the scrappy main harvest was done and winter wasn't far away when Juleen came to me. I was washing my hands after feeding the pigs and she smiled in a way that she had smiled all her life except that there was no heart in it and there hadn't been since she'd come back. Her smile was like a hat she could put on and take off at any time and it meant no more to her than that. 'Those shimmerflowers,' she said brushing some dirt off my sleeve. 'The ones you brought me on my Day. Where did you say they came from?'

I shook the water from my hands. 'I thought you said you couldn't remember anything from your Day.'

Juleen's companion glanced around with quick sharp movements. Juleen stroked it. 'Little things have come back to me. Bits and pieces.'

'The monster?'

Did her eyes narrow just a little? She pinched my cheek and her companion scuttled from her far shoulder to the one nearest me. 'Silly. There was no monster.'

'There was. It ate you.'

'If it ate me, how is it I'm here?'

I shook my head. 'I know what I saw.'

'Poor Panny. It must have been a shock, my disappearing like that. You're all mixed up.'

'I know what I saw.'

'Shimmerflowers,' she repeated as if I had said nothing at all, 'I feel the need for some shimmerflowers.'

Juleen wanted me to go with her up to the crag. I didn't want to, not with this new Juleen, but she led the way and I followed.

The crag was sharp ridges among sharp ridges, broken rocks and hardness, with a few little pockets where the shimmerflowers grow. I took her there but I couldn't find any of the flowers. I looked hard but she didn't at all.

Juleen stood on the highest point of the crag, the broken spine that looked all the way down to the river valley. While her companion clung to the back of her neck, she held her arms wide and closed her eyes. 'Come and stand with me!' she cried barefoot and open. 'Feel the world!'

I grumbled but I scrambled after her. Her dress flapped and snapped around her and her hair streamed like a flag. She raised her voice over the wind. 'You have no companion!'

'I'm not sixteen!'

'Would you like one?'

'Everyone wants a companion.'

Juleen's companion scurried down her arm and sat in her cradled hands. 'Oh yes,' Juleen said. 'Everyone wants a companion.'

The wind howled and I wanted to too. 'Why are you changed?'

'We all change.'

'That's not what I mean and you know it. You came back and you're different.'

'How?'

'I've seen you smiling and talking to your thing and happy when other people's companions have gone.'

'I thought you may have,' she said, and she pushed me off the ridge.

* * *

Old Marda's sparrow found me. Old Marda swore and cursed as she carried my broken body back to her hut. 'Stupid, stupid,' she muttered. 'Stupid, stupid.'

Pain wrapped me up tightly and held me for a long, long time. 'Stupid, stupid,' was a drumbeat in my brain. 'Stupid, stupid.'

A time came when I could open my eyes without wanting to die. Old Marda was at my side sitting on a three-legged stool. Her hair stood out on her head grey and straw like. Her stone sparrow peered at me cocking its head from side to side. 'You fell on soft ground. You're lucky.'

'Lucky?' I croaked. I sounded like I was eight thousand years old.

'Shimmerflowers were under your head. Cushioned it. That's what I call luck.'

I nodded and the world went away.

I woke more often after that and even began eating. Old Marda hadn't told Ma and Da. Not safe, she said.

I got to know the inside of that hut very well from my pallet on the floor. I was surprised. It was very clean. Bunches of herbs hung from the beams. The small hearth must have had a good chimney since no smoke lingered inside. She kept a small vase with flowers and changed them when they wilted. Red latners. Pink shallashades. The tiny yellow dot lilies.

We ate well but no fish, not ever.

'Why did she do it?' I asked one day when it was raining outside.

Old Marda didn't ask who I meant. 'We'll never know.'

'What?'

'Some things have no answers.'

I thought about that for some time before saying, 'She tried to kill me.'

'I'm not surprised.'

* * *

Old Marda made me walk even when it hurt. Four paces up, four paces back, the whole length of the hut. She gave me rocks wrapped in cloth and made me lift them up and down, up and down, until I was strong.

One night I was shaken awake. 'We've got something to show you,' Old Marda said.

It was the first time I had set foot outside the hut. The night was warm as soup. I stood for a while staring at the clouds and the stars that peeped out between them. 'How long has it been?' I asked Old Marda.

'Four months, more or less.'

'So much sky. So much world.'

'Time for that later.' Old Marda's companion appeared fluttering out of the night sky and perched on her shoulder. It peeped out at me with bird bright eyes then it flew off again. Old Marda nodded and scowled. She took my arm and we followed her companion through the trees to the village.

We passed the back of a few houses until Old Marda tugged on my arm and we dropped crouching. Old Marda pointed at the figure that was crawling through the scrub behind Amtalla's house. Something scuttled up the side of the house, hoisted itself onto the roof and burrowed through the thatch. In a minute the shutters inched open and the figure in the garden stood up.

Juleen.

I started to go to her but Old Marda grabbed me and slapped a hand over my mouth to stop me crying out. I struggled for a moment then Juleen's companion dragged a limp flufftypup out of the window.

I made a noise, a tiny hopeless sound. 'Amtalla's companion,' Old Marda whispered.

Juleen took the flufftypup. Her mouth opened wider and wider, her jaw almost touching her chest. She ate the flufftypup whole.

I crumpled into Old Marda's arms as Juleen wiped her mouth with both hands. Her companion leapt from the windowsill to her shoulder and pawed at her lips. And she stroked it and sank into the scrub and wormed away.

Old Marda held me for a long time before releasing her grip. 'How many?' I asked. My legs ached.

'Apart from your mother and father, that was the last.'

'All of them? Everyone in the village?'

'Dead, or as near as maybe. Your folks have taken in the children who were orphaned, all six of them.'

'Juleen?'

'As worried and as anxious as your parents.'

'Is she?'

'I don't think so, but that's how she appears.'

'She eats companions.'

'She does. She's very hungry.'

* * *

Old Marda helped me back to her hut. My legs hurt, my back hurt and my heart hurt most of all.

Old Marda gasped. Juleen was standing on her doorstep.

'You two.' She wagged a finger at us and her companion wagged a furry limb. 'You're always watching, aren't you?'

'Juleen,' I wailed. 'What's happened to you?'

She bounced off the step towards us. 'Lots of things. Lots of things happen when you get eaten by a monster.'

Old Marda waved her skinny arms. 'Go away! Leave us alone!'

'Oh, I can't that. I'm so dreadfully hungry.'

Juleen's companion sprang. Old Marda's stone sparrow chirped and fluttered into the air and barely escaped the horrid thing. It landed on Old Marda. She screeched and tried to knock it off but it held on. While

Juleen laughed it hissed and slashed at Old Marda's arm with its gutting claws. The stone sparrow chirped frantically and circled overhead but Old Marda staggered and fell before I could catch her.

Juleen's companion scuttled over. Juleen scooped it up and placed it on her shoulder and she clapped and laughed. 'Such clever venom! And we'll have that stone sparrow soon, I'm sure.'

She turned her attention to me and it was like standing in front of one of the baker's ovens. 'You didn't stay dead. Good.'

'Good?'

'There's not much left to eat. Once we've had that stone sparrow then it's just the growlbear and the patchy left.'

'Ma and Da's companions? You can't!'

'Oh, I can.' She licked her lips but then her face fell and she held her horrible companion up to her face. 'But then we'll have no more to eat and I'm getting hungrier and hungrier!'

It chittered at her and waved its arms. A slow smile spread across Juleen's face and she looked at me. 'What a good idea!'

I moaned. 'No, Juleen, no.'

'But I have to, little brother. Don't you see that?'

'No!'

I turned and hobbled away as best I could. I'd find Ma and Da. I'd tell them what happened. I'd show them Old Marda. I'd make them believe.

Juleen followed me. She walked slowly and juggled her companion from hand to hand. 'You're awfully slow. That fall must have broken lots of bones.'

I didn't answer. I was already gasping and I needed to save my breath. I hurried on even though my hips hurt and I had red hot pokers in my shoes.

'You can't hide,' Juleen called. I looked back. She wasn't there. I turned around and there she was a stone's throw away standing between me and our house. 'I'll eat you first and then I'll eat them.' She frowned. 'After that, I suppose I'll have to start on the trees and the rocks. Hungrier and hungrier, that's me!'

Her companion was on top of her head and it danced a jerky and horrible dance. I cried out and stumbled off.

I got to the village square. The rock was tall and shadowy in front of me. My chest was a bundle of hot pain. I reached the rock and held myself up against it.

Juleen's voice ran around the square echoing off the empty houses and workshops. 'I can see you!'

I wanted to cry and I stuffed my fist in my mouth so I wouldn't make a noise. She was going to take me and her awful companion was going to poison me and I was going to lie in the dark for years. And when it came to my Day it would be a nightmare Day.

I found the ladder and dragged myself up rung by rung to the top of the rock. I was breaking every sacred rule there ever was but it was better than what Juleen had in store for me. Juleen? Was it Juleen? Whatever she was she wasn't my sister.

On top of the rock I lay on my back and panted. Thick clouds, no stars. I was alone but I was on top of the rock.

I rolled over. The rock wasn't flat. It had bumps and scoops and it had the stone crown. We called it a crown even though it was a simple ring made out of the same stone as the rock. No writing. No pattern. Just stone. I reached for it but Juleen came to the top of the ladder. 'There you are!'

I moaned and crawled away until I was right on the edge. Juleen hopped onto the rock and clapped her hands together. 'We're up so high!'

'Juleen, don't.'

She frowned. 'I'm sorry. I don't know where Juleen has gone.'

She hummed a little tune and wandered over to the stone crown. She nudged it with her toe. 'What a silly thing.'

She pointed at me. Her companion scuttled off her shoulder down her arm and darted at me.

I wailed but it leapt at me. I kicked as hard as I could. I got it fair and square but instead of falling off the edge of the rock it just tumbled back a little and landed right next to Juleen.

Old Marda's stone sparrow fluttered out of the night sky. It opened its beak and dropped a shimmerflower at Juleen's feet.

She stared at the shimmerflower. She picked it up and stared at it and her face cleared and the old Juleen peeped out. 'I loved shimmerflowers,' she whispered.

'You did.'

'I loved you.'

'Juleen,' I said. 'You're back?'

'Panny?'

'Help me.'

The furry thing reared up on its hind legs and waved it claws and chattered at her. Juleen kicked at it but it slashed at her bare feet. She cried out and then grabbed the stone crown. The creature rushed at her and Juleen swung the crown like a sickle. When she hit the creature, she turned to sand, the creature turned to sand, and the whole world turned to sand.

* * *

Morning. The sun was in my face. Old Marda was squinting at me. 'You're tougher than you look,' she croaked.

'So are you. Aren't you dead?'

'Sick as a slant rat, but not dead. That thing must have used up most of its venom before it got to me.'

I sat up. We were in the square but the rock was gone. Where it had been was a huge mound of sand. I shook my head. The rock couldn't be gone. It was always there. 'What happened?'

'I was hoping you could tell me.'

I told her about Juleen and her companion and how they chased me. 'Juleen saved me, though.'

'At the last, she remembered who she was.'

'She didn't kill me.'

'Maybe not everything is trying to kill us.'

Old Marda took me back to Ma and Da. They cried a lot and they welcomed Old Marda and they thanked her. After that she was part of our family, with the six littlies. We were all that was left. Life was hard but we went on living because that's what you do even with no companions and with souls that will never be safe.

The Author: Michael Pryor

Michael Pryor is one of Australia's most popular and acclaimed authors of fantasy and science fiction. He has published more than thirty-five novels (including the Laws of Magic series, *Machine Wars* and *10 Futures*) more than fifty short stories, and has over one million words in print. His work has been longlisted for an Inky award, shortlisted for the WAYBR award and seven times shortlisted for the Aurealis Award. Seven of his books have been awarded Children's Book Council of Australia Notable Book status. His latest book is *Leo da Vinci Vs the Ice-cream Domination League*. His website is michaelpryor.com.au.

Story Behind the Story

When I finish writing a book, I like to turn my mind to something completely different. For instance, if I've just finished writing a steampunk book, I'll have a go at a far future robot story. In this case, I'd just finished writing a contemporary comedic supernatural book and, to refresh myself, I felt like writing a horror/weird story, with lots of uncanny uncertainties, as well as a naïve, child narrator for extra creepiness. Thus, 'Shimmerflowers'.

The Illustrator: Kim Lennard

Kim Lennard is a freelance digital artist who has a love for all forms of artwork especially fantasy art. Kim creates her images using a combination of photos, textures and digital painting with Photoshop CS6 and an intuous5 tablet. Kim lives in Newcastle, Australia and undertakes commission artworks for both the literature and music industry. Kim is known as kimsol in the deviantART community and can be contacted there directly at kimsol.deviantart.com.

Illustration by Matt Bissett-Johnson

The Mandelbrot Bet

Dirk Strasser

'There are lines which are monsters.'

Eugène Delacroix

Voice notes to self on the development of the escape-time algorithm—
Daniel Rostrom

Remember, the answer is always simple. That's not to say the simple answer is the correct one. The danger to avoid is the assumption that the simple answer, by the sole nature of its simplicity, is correct.

The escape-time algorithm is the simplest algorithm for generating a representation of the Mandelbrot set. The answer lies in the infinity of the escape-time algorithm. Repeat the calculation for each x, y, z, t point and make your decisions based on the behaviour of that calculation. Pick a value for time, t, square it, add a constant. Take the new number, square it, and add the same constant. Forever, do it forever. Simple.

'Give me a moment before you shove any more of that stuff in my mouth.'
'Sorry, Daniel, it's hard for me to guess when you're ready for another spoonful.'

'You asked me a question, so give me a chance to answer it.'

'You must have gotten stuck today. You're always grumpy when you get stuck.'

'And you're the only one here I can be grumpy with, Helen. Sorry, it's because I can't move my body that it gets to me when I can't get my mind moving as well.'

'All right, how about having another go at explaining to me what you were thinking about today? Even if I don't understand it, it may help you gain some insight.'

'I suppose there's always a chance. Okay, do you remember what I was saying about the Mandelbrot set and how I've developed the idea to include a time dimension?'

'Er, yes, I remember good old Benoît B Mandelbrot. French, wasn't he?'

'No, technically Lithuanian. Lived and worked most of his life in the US, but that's not really important, is it?'

'I just like a bit of a context.'

'Okay, well the important thing is I've tied the behaviour of Mandelbrot-like time dimensions to quantum computing.'

'Here, eat this before you go on. I need a moment to digest what you've said.'

'Ha ha.'

'Just chew on this, Daniel.'

The loner in physics—Eleanora Schmidt

Is it possible for a non-physics trained person to make a fundamental breakthrough in physics? Does nature speak in a language that an intelligent, determined non-specialist can decipher? Self-taught artists can sometimes create something truly extraordinary that a fully trained artist can't. It can be argued that the training itself limits thought patterns and inhibits creative leaps.

The loner physicist has the added handicap that he or she is not working as part of a team. Are great discoveries still achievable by individuals working alone? Some would argue that this is still possible. A case in point is the work of Daniel Rostrom, a man with little formal physics training who brought his skills from other fields such as computer science, art, and geography to bear on the complex field of time travel speculation.

The jury is still out whether Daniel Rostrom was the greatest polymath and deepest thinker of our century, a brilliant hoaxer, or a fringe-dwelling crackpot. Rostrom, whose muscular dystrophy meant he was wheelchair-bound for much of his life, presents us with the most detailed insight into the loner physicist. As a young man he had a bionic recording device implanted into his brain that he could switch on and off at will. The original intention was to use it to play podcasts of scientific papers that he would otherwise have physical difficulty in reading and to keep a verbal record of his thoughts. In practice he kept the device recording most of the time with a cloud-sync to his computerised chair, so we have a full record of everything he said and heard. The latter recordings, which are dated after his disappearance, are the subject of much debate. Most in the scientific community believe them to be an elaborate hoax, but there are those who believe they are genuine. The question always arises, as to how a wheelchair-bound man with late-stage muscular dystrophy could simply disappear without his caregiver or any family members having any idea where he had gone. There are, of course, myriad conspiracy theories, but there are also physicists who have argued cogently that the most likely series of events was that he simply did what he said he would do.

'That's not what you said last time, Helen.'

'So now you're going to play back my words again, are you Daniel? Just to make me look bad.'

'No. I don't want to make you look bad.'

'Look, Daniel, that bionic recorder drives me insane. Can't you turn it off for conversations with me?'

'I could, but it would make it harder to get to the truth.'

'I might just quit. How would you like that sort of truth?'

'You've said that…'

'Don't give me a precise count of how often I've said I'd quit.'

'I'm sorry, Helen. I never mean to upset you.'

'Being your full-time caregiver isn't a picnic, and it's not exactly pleasant when you have a digitised record of everything I've ever said to you inside your head.'

'You know I'm after the truth. What else have I got sitting here in this wheelchair with nothing but numbness below my neck?'

'Yes, well you stick to scientific truth. The rest of us only have the fuzzy truth we deal with day to day.'

'There's only one sort of truth, Helen.'

'And you're going to find it.'

'That's right, I'm going to find it.'

Voice notes to self on the development of the escape-time algorithm— *Daniel Rostrom*

One of two things always happens in a Mandelbrot set: either an iterated point jumps up to two units away from the origin or it jumps further away. The result is a shape that is finite but an edge that is infinite. It's all about the edge. The line. It's a monster. The more you magnify it, the more complex it becomes. It never settles down. Ever. I know this is the key. Somehow a Mandelbrot set has only two dimensions, yet it also possesses another dimension. What if that other dimension was time? With the right procedure it must be possible to both orbit close to an origin and jump in ever-increasing spans. I know I'm onto something. Think.

This isn't just a computer-generated image, it's real life. Coastlines. You can see it in coastlines. They're infinitely long. Magnify them and you will see more twists and kinks. Magnify them again, and you see even more. It never stops.

There is no arrow of time. It's a coastline of time.

'So, this chair of yours is going to be your so-called time machine?'

'Like in the HG Wells novel. Except it won't be coming with me. You've only just realised that, Helen?'

'I'm a bit slow, remember? You've often told me that.'

'No, I haven't. I can prove—'

'Don't worry about calling up the relevant recordings. Even if you haven't said it, I feel it from you sometimes.'

'Do you really?'

'Never mind. Tell me again how this is going to work.'

'Could you keep massaging my scalp while I do?'

'All right.'

'I mean sometimes you stop massaging when you're thinking.'

'I promise I won't think.'

'Very amusing.'

'Can you start explaining?'

'It's all about uncertainty.'

'Mmm, all right, go on.'

'You've switched off already, haven't you?'

'No, but I know you're using the word *uncertainty* in that way you always use words. I'll bet it's not the way most of us use the word.'

'Okay… think of it like a *bet*. You know how in a horse race, you can never be absolutely certain of which horse will win?'

'Unless the race is fixed and I'm in on the fix.'

'Unless the race is fixed. Can we assume it's not fixed?'

'Of course, it's your race. So we can't be sure of which horse will win?'

'Yes, we don't know anything for certain, but people who know what they're doing assign odds of winning to each horse.'

'So do people who don't know what they're doing.'

'Are you going to let me continue?'

'You're not telling me anything I don't know, Daniel.'

'I'm trying to simplify it.'

'For my slow brain.'

'I told you I've never said you have a slow—'

'Look, Daniel, just go on.'

'Well, the escape-time algorithm I've been working on comes down to writing a computer program into my chair that uses the uncertainty in the four-dimensional extension to the Mandelbrot set principle I've been extrapolating.'

'I see.'

'A horse race is based on mild randomness. Things like height and weight also have a mild random distribution. You're not going to come across a twenty-metre-tall person all of a sudden, for example. Mandelbrot set-like behaviour is based on *wild* randomness.'

'So in the Mandelbrot world twenty-metre-tall people are common?'

'Not exactly. But there are lots of examples of Mandelbrot set-like distributions in the real world. Nearly all human-made variables are wild. Wealth, for example, is a wild variable. We have a number of individuals that have millions of times more wealth than the average person. We live in a winner-take-all world of extremes.'

'See, this is why I like hearing about your work, Daniel.'

'Can you keep massaging?'

'Sorry, you caught me thinking.'

'Look at Babble. It controls ninety percent of the cloud traffic. And who's the latest best-selling enhanced fiction author?'

'It's probably—'

'Never mind, it was a rhetorical question. I'll guarantee you that whoever she is, she earns millions more than the vast majority of enhanced fiction authors. And she won't be millions times better than those other authors.'

'No, but she's pretty good.'

'Are you deliberately sidetracking me?'

'Yes, sorry.'

'Anyway, what I'm doing is using wild randomness to accelerate myself into an extreme future time period. And because of the wildness, I can't be absolutely certain what the Mandelbrot set-like variables will do to me.'

'So, it's sort of like a Mandelbrot *bet*?'

Voice notes to self on the development of the escape-time algorithm— *Daniel Rostrom*

I've found what I've been overlooking. Possibility theory. It describes the uncertainty that I've been missing. It's the only way to deal with extreme probabilities and partial ignorance. I need to look at both the possibility and necessity of the event. If the universe is finite (which we know it is) and every subset of it is measurable (which is what everything we do in science is based on), then the universe describes all possible future states of the world. Obvious now. Outcomes aren't self-dual. I need to stop thinking with two-valued logic and start thinking with multi-valued logic.

'Nǐ tīngdǒng ma?'

'What?'

'We're sorry, our records say Mandarin Chinese was the most common language in your space–time period. It was a statistical guess that you would understand it. Shall we proceed with mid-twenty-first-century English? Is that convenient for you, doctor?'

'Doctor?'

'That is the correct form of address, is it not, for a scientist from your space–time period?'

'I don't have doctorate. My name is Daniel Rostrom. What... what space–time period am I in?'

'It depends what scale you use. Allow me to elucidate, Mr Rostrom.'

'Please do.'

'You understand something of the life-cycle of stars?'

'Of course. It's not my major interest, but I know my cosmology.'

'Do you see—we use the word *see* as an approximation, of course—do you see the white light in your vision?'

'Yes, in fact, that's all I can see.'

'You would be aware that neutron stars, black holes, and black dwarfs are dead stars. What you see here is a white dwarf, a star that, although still alive, is dying. This low-mass white dwarf will become dimmer and dimmer until it fades into a black dwarf. Do you know what a black dwarf is?'

'Yes, it emits no electromagnetic radiation. Black dwarfs were only theoretical in the mid-twenty-first century. They couldn't exist because the time taken for a white dwarf to cool to such a degree was longer than the lifespan of the universe up to my time period.'

'We will talk about time in a moment. The important thing to appreciate is that a white dwarf can sustain life, a black dwarf can't.'

'But white dwarfs can also evolve into supernovae.'

'Exactly my point. *High-mass* white dwarfs become supernovae and the expanding shock waves from these explosions form new stars. This is how the life-cycle of the universe functions. Death. Life. Death. Life.'

'But you said this white dwarf has a small mass, so it's going to die and become a black dwarf.'

'Precisely, Mr Rostrom, but there is something you must understand now. What you have seen here is the last star of its kind.'

'The last white dwarf?'

'Yes, the last white dwarf in a universe, which for billions upon billions of years has contained only white dwarfs and dead stars.'

'Now, you *are* telling me something I don't understand. There are countless yellow dwarfs, red giants, and brown dwarfs in our universe.'

'There *were*. A long time ago. For eons the only stars in the universe still clinging onto life have been white dwarfs. And now there is only one remaining.'

'What?'

'I believe we began our conversation with that question.'

Voice notes to self on the development of the escape-time algorithm— *Daniel Rostrom*

It's just a matter of applying the right iterative algorithm to time travel. Quantum computers are powerful enough to do it and quantum computers don't get much more powerful than my chair. I just have to get the sequence of qubits right. Of course I don't know for certain what will happen, but possibility theory tells me the likelihood.

'I think I understand. The escape-time algorithm has inevitably brought me here to the end of the universe as limiting asymptote. I'm here, so close to the end. The last white star about to go black. The last skerrick of life about to be extinguished, but I will never quite reach it.'

'That would be true if your quantum leaps were still occurring, but they're not. You're now in real-time, and the end is imminent.'

'So I'm going to see the universe end?'

'Technically, your mind will be extinguished a nanosecond before it happens, but yes, unless we can find a solution, you will see the universe die.'

'A solution?'

'Sentient beings, no matter how advanced, never want to be extinguished. We will continue striving for an escape solution until the very end.'

'You keep saying *we*. Who are the others?'

'We are speaking to you in what you would call one voice, but there are countless beings here. We have unified. There are no individuals any more. There haven't been any for several million years. We've evolved into a single entity. Our knowledge is shared.'

'One entity. That's all that's left?'

'Yes. At a point in our universes' history a sentient race evolved to achieve unity, to become a single sentient being, possessing the sum total of knowledge and understanding that each individual had.'

'What happened to the other races?'

'As eons passed, other sentient races came to the same point in their evolution and first unified as a race and then joined us. As it became clear that the universe was dying, the main aim of sentient beings was to find ways to prolong its life, or at least to find a way of prolonging sentient life. Those beings that had not joined us knew that they now had no choice. The only hope for us all was to collectively put all our knowledge into solving the ultimate problem. That is what we have been doing for millions of years. And it is what we continue to do even now.'

'But there must be others here now, if what you say about the escape-time algorithm is correct. It's impossible that no-one else ever discovered what I discovered. In the billions of years of the history of the universe and the countless sentient beings, there must be other time travellers who found their way here to the end of the universe?'

'There have been others that have arrived here through the process you discovered. Many others. They are already here with us as part of the unified entity.

'You've… assimilated them?'

'Of course.'

'And you think you're going to assimilate me as well?'

'Our last best hope is that assimilating your mind will enable us to devise a solution to stop the last white dwarf turning black. You are the last time traveller. No-one will arrive after you. There is no time anymore.'

'I… don't want to be assimilated. I've always worked alone. My thoughts are my own.'

'You have no choice, Mr Rostrom.'

'You can't take my mind. It's all I have.'

'It's all *we* have.'

'Let me stay separate. Please, I can solve the problem myself. Just give me the knowledge you have. I came here to the end of the universe without anyone's help. I can get us out of this.'

'There is no form of logic that would suggest that is true. We calculate that the possibility quotient of us finding a way to escape our fate, although extremely low, is higher if your mind is assimilated with ours.'

'Wait. You said I'm the last to arrive—true?'

'Yes.'

'The escape-time algorithm produces iterations in inverse proportion to the start time period. If I'm the last to arrive, then I must have been the first in the history of the universe to discover the escape-time algorithm.'

'Yes, you are very astute, but—'

'So, there is something special about me. Others had more advanced knowledge to work with than I did. What I have done is the least possible of all time travel events.'

'Correct, but—'

'I think I've argued a strong case for remaining an individual. Please give me everything you know and maybe I'll help us escape the end of the universe.'

Voice notes to self on the development of the escape-end-universe algorithm— Daniel Rostrom

The universe is dying. The entity has enabled sense simulation for me. I asked for a simulated body while I worked on the new algorithm, and I look like an Adonis. For the first time in my life I can feel what it's like to be physically powerful. I flex my muscles and can't stop laughing as I sift through the information and threads of reasoning the entity is feeding me. If only I had more time. I know I can find a solution. Or is that just idiotic arrogance? There's a thought I've never had before. Maybe with the freedom of my new body I've finally become aware of my limitations. Wouldn't that be ironic? Helen, you've probably noticed these aren't proper voice notes anymore. I'm really talking to you—you know that, don't you?

'The time has come, Daniel. Everything is now too late. Do you want to join us for the end?'

'No, I want face it alone.'

'You continue to surprise us with your choices.'

'Well, that's what life is all about, isn't it? With only one sentient being in the universe, where are the surprises?'

'There are no more surprises. We've both failed.'

'I'm going to keep reporting what I see.'

'Of course.'

'Will anyone hear?'

'That's beyond even our abilities to know. Theoretically quantum synapses on your neural link may make it possible. You have been very astute, but the time distortions cannot be mapped by any algorithm.'

'Not astute enough to come up with a way to stop the universe from ending.'

'I believe it's happening now.'

'What, so soon?'

'You persist in your time perceptions.'

Helen, I can feel the wild stellar winds buffet me as a bright shimmer appears in my vision. The white mass of the last living star in the universe is beginning to shed its outer layers. It's so beautiful. I wish you could see it with me. Inside I can see a crystalline lattice of carbon and oxygen atoms, a diamond-like core glowing with intense light.

Now it's all starting to darken.

Helen, if you can still hear me, I want to say goodbye. I know I didn't always treat you as well as I should have. I'm... I'm going to say something I thought I would take to my grave. I'm so gutless I can only say it now because possibility theory suggests it's highly unlikely that you'll ever hear it. Helen, I've always loved you. I know you couldn't ever love such a twisted cripple as me, so I chose never to say anything. I recorded all our conversations not to trip you up about things you had said in the past, but because I never wanted your voice to leave me. That's the real truth. Goodbye, my truth.'

The loner in physics—*Eleanora Schmidt*

Daniel Rostrom's recordings, therefore, are either delusional flights of fancy that will keep the world's psychiatrists busy for decades to come or they present the scientific community with unsurpassed information and reasoning about the end of the universe. Who knows, perhaps by giving one sentient race such depth of understanding so early in the life of the universe, perhaps we have the head start we need, and in the billions of years until the end, the sentient beings of the universe will learn enough to stop the death of the last star.

'Daniel, I guess I'm hoping you're so brilliant that you've somehow engineered it so that you can still hear me. If not, well, I guess I'm just talking to myself here. I have been listening to every word. People think you're making it all up, but I believe you. I believe everything you've said. I do love you too. And I could have loved you more if you'd let me. Believing you, of course, means you'll never come back. You won the bet. Well done. Goodbye, Daniel.'

The Author: Dirk Strasser

Dirk Strasser has won multiple Australian Publisher Association Awards and a Ditmar for Best Professional Achievement. His short story 'The Doppelgänger Effect' appeared in the World Fantasy Award-winning anthology, *Dreaming Down Under*. His fiction—including his fantasy trilogy *The Books of Ascension: Zenith*, *Equinox* and *Eclipse*, and the stories in his collection, *Stories of the Sand*—has been translated into a number of languages. He founded the Aurealis Awards and has co-published and co-edited *Aurealis* magazine for over 25 years. His website is at dirkstrasser.com.

Story Behind the Story

The twin origins of this story were an article on fractals and a title in search of a story. I often have the title of a story before anything else. When I was contacted by Eric Choi to submit to the Tor hard SF anthology, *Carbide Tipped Pens*, which he was co-editing with Ben Bova, I immediately thought of 'The Mandelbrot Bet' title. The result is my humble attempt to write the ultimate hard SF time-travel love story, where non-Gaussian randomness, Possibility Theory and Cosmology combine to save the universe.

The Illustrator: Matt Bissett-Johnson

Matt Bissett-Johnson is a freelance cartoonist, caricature artist, illustrator and animator. His work can be seen at mattbj.blogspot.com and mbjsgeekyfreak.blogspot.com.

Illustration by Peter Allert

The Bewitching of Dr Travidian (A Romance)

Geoffrey Maloney

Prologue: Armadillo Man

A lean young man, dressed far too elegantly for the neighbourhood he was in, staggered along a narrow street of sad rickety houses. He held a handkerchief scented with rosewater to his nose to guard against the odours of the open sewer. With barely enough moonlight to guide his way, he would stop occasionally and squint at the numbers scrawled in chalk upon the doors, mumble to himself, then move on.

A sound from behind sent his heart racing and brought a sudden sobriety to his gin-soaked head. Spinning round, he was relieved to find nothing more than an armadillo scratching in a pile of refuse. 'Ah, my sweet and pretty thing,' he cooed. The scaly beast gave him a menacing look with its paint-drop eyes then shot between his legs and into the oily blackness of the sewer. Thrown off balance, the young man clutched at the nearest door. He put his eye up close to it. Yes, this was the one. Surely it was fate that had sent the armadillo his way. He rapped out the code he'd been given by the drunken sailor at the Chicken Whistle Inn.

Three taps, two taps, three taps more. He waited, breathing slowly to steady himself; perhaps she was… but, no, the old salt had said the Senora never sleeps, and her magic always works. When the door opened, barely an inch or two, he whispered his request and, with a trembling hand, pushed an envelope containing six silver dollars through the dark crack

The door closed. Several slow minutes passed. He began to feel anxious, fearful for his life once more. Then the creaking of a hinge and the envelope without its coins was returned to him. He hurried away, his heart beating rapidly, but his head clearing, as if all the anxiety he'd felt had purged the gin from his body.

Beneath the first flickering gas lamp, he stopped briefly. Moths with singed wings fluttered above his head and mosquitoes planted blood kisses upon his neck. Peeling the envelope open, he found a soft grey powder inside, and a slip of paper upon which instructions had been written in a shaky hand. The smell that came to his nostrils was reminiscent of saltpetre. It would burn. It would cast a spell among the flames.

Part I: One Stripe or Two

Dr David Travidian was a tall thin man of perhaps twenty-eight with a growing reputation as a scholar and teacher of the classics. Just now, he stood gazing out his study window down into the school quadrangle, trying to ignore the hangover that had robbed him of his intellect for most of the day. She was there, Cassandra Ignatius, an elegant figure in grey silk standing beneath the old jacaranda tree, awaiting the release of her brother from yet another detention.

Travidian felt the full swelling of the melancholia that had engulfed him since his first casual glimpse of her at the school fair. Melancholia? No, he thought, forlorn it was he felt, and Love-forlornness was the folly that rode him.

Travidian turned from the window to the boy who sat before his desk with his head bowed. 'I am feeling somewhat benevolent this evening, Master Alexander. You do not like receiving stripes. It may surprise you to find that I do not like giving them, but give them I will unless your behaviour improves in my classroom. Do you understand?'

Master Alexander Ignatius nodded. He was a stocky lad, with a strong and noble nose, perhaps just a little too large for his face, but he had the same deep dark eyes as his sister.

'So, a test instead,' Travidian said, picking his cane up from his desk and running the tempered bamboo shaft through his fingers, 'and if you answer correctly there shall be no stripes.'

The boy nodded.

'Please name the Seven Follies of the Clown.'

The humidity of the evening had crept in through the open window. Beads of sweat were gathering upon both their brows.

'The Clown, sir?'

'Yes, *the* Clown.'

'Please, sir, I don't think we have studied him in class yet.'

'That is correct. We have not. But you have been doing your reading, have you not? It is on your list. It is why the school has a library. You can't be spending all your time on the sports. Not in this weather. Come now, at least tell me his name. Everyone knows it, if only from his street pantomimes.'

The boy remained silent. He knew he should know the name. Indeed, he believed he had once known it, seen it, read it somewhere, but it seemed he'd failed to pack his memory that morning, so anxious he'd been to get to the cricket field.

Dr Travidian stared directly ahead. A minute ticked away. 'Please stand up.'

Master Alexander rose from the chair and stuck his hand out. Dr Travidian flexed the cane, swung it high. It hovered there for a moment, and Alexander thought he was about to be given a reprieve, but then it came whistling down. It bit into the soft flesh of his fingers, stinging like a wasp. The boy sucked in his breath, shook his hand, and closed his eyes to squeeze out the pain.

'The Clown's name was Joseph Hilarious,' Dr Travidian said. 'At least that is what he called himself, and no scholar yet has been able to prove whether it was his true name or merely another example of his humour. So knowing his name it should come as no surprise to you that the first folly is Hilarity. Silly disruptive laughter for the sake of it. Which is what you so excellently illustrated in my classroom today. The second folly is Gastronomy, not to be confused with Gluttony, which is one of the Seven Sins. With respect to Gastronomy, Joseph Hilarious once came upon a prominent chef separating eggs. To make meringue and flummery. The Clown said in his usual manner: "It is an egg, my good fellow! Boil it, peel it and eat it! Perhaps with a little salt and pepper, and be done with it." Come now, this must ring some bells.'

Alexander shook his head. He raised his other hand stoically for the second stripe, but the doctor placed his cane upon the desk. He sat down in his chair, steepled his fingers over his nose and gazed at his pupil. Now was the time for his folly.

'Sit down,' Dr Travidian said, opening his desk drawer. From it he took a jar of arnica, and pushed it towards the boy.

Alexander took some of the dark green unguent and massaged it into his stinging fingers.

'Look to your left, young man. Directly on the shelf there you will find a book about Hilarious the Clown. It is one I wrote myself. You may borrow it. I expect you to read and study it well.'

Master Alexander Ignatius's eyes grew wide. No more stripes. He reached towards the shelf, but the master's cane was in his hand once more. This time it came down gently, a barrier between the boy and the book.

'There is just one small thing,' Travidian said, 'to seal our bargain. Let's see how adventurous and clever you are, as well as how studious you might prove to be. It is a challenge I'm setting you, a very special and secret one. Are you up for it?'

Master Alexander looked at the book, then looked at the cane. He nodded. 'Yes, sir.'

'Very well, your goal over the next two days is to take three hairs from your sister's bed. Do you think you can manage that, to prove to me that you are the man I think you are? Now take the book. You are released from detention. I will walk down with you.'

The boy hesitated.

'What is it?' Travidian asked.

'As I do not share a room with my sister, sir, and father has forbidden me to enter her room that task may not be an easy one.'

'Precisely why I have set it as a challenge for you. You will find a way. That is all part of it.' Travidian tapped his forehead. 'Careful thinking and planning must come before the action, yes?'

Travidian allowed Alexander to walk before him as they descended the stairs and entered the quadrangle. Here the humidity was even thicker, the air was warm and stifling damp against the skin, like a coil of rope drawn into the lungs. And there she was, Cassandra Ignatius, with her face hidden fashionably behind a delicate veil. She had lifted it at the school fete last month. It was that glimpse of her face, naked in the sunlight, that had started his infatuation.

'I adore you,' Travidian wished to say, as he bowed and kissed her hand.

Cassandra Ignatius drew away quickly, and hid her hand amongst the voluptuous silk of her frock, where Travidian imagined she rubbed away the touch of his unworthy lips. Then with only a slight nod of her head, she swept her brother to her skirts, scurried away across the quadrangle, and onto the street where their carriage waited.

Too proud, too noble, and far too wealthy, Travidian thought. He should not have kissed her hand. It had been presumptuous of him. A bow would have been enough, but then she had offered her hand, had she not?

Part II: Crushed Strawberries

Having read to her brother and prayed with him for the Lord their mother's soul to keep, Cassandra Ignatius descended the stairs to take her seat at the dinner table, ready to play the gracious hostess for her father's business associates. She was resplendent as she entered the dining room in a gown of crushed strawberry silk. Its hem swept the polished floor with a delicate swish, and as she crossed to the table, one of the gentleman, Mr Sevigny she believed, leapt up and bowed awkwardly. He was one of the 'waverers' her father had mentioned and, no doubt, he had been promised much. She could imagine what he was thinking right then, as he pulled her chair out for her. A soft flush rose to her cheeks.

As she took her seat, she smiled politely at her father sitting at the opposite end of the table. He returned her smile, cast his eyes quickly around and gave her a wink. 'Gentleman, the beauty of my household graces us with her presence. Please drink to my daughter's health.'

The seating arrangements were as strategic as her father's gaze had suggested. Mr Ranger, the young scientist and member of the Academy had been placed in the centre on her father's right. He was keen, as everyone knew, to mount an expedition of a joint scientific and mercantile nature to the southern seas. Directly opposite him, was Captain Applegate, recently retired from the royal navy, but determined to have one more adventure upon the high seas. Both of these men where what her father called 'believers'.

To the immediate left and right of her father were the 'doubters': Sir Thomas and Dr Ryder. Both were yet to be convinced of the expedition's worth. To her own left was the gracious Mr Sevigny. He was a pleasant looking young man, in his early twenties, and heir to his family's wine estates. To her right was Lord Eccles, a man of considerable wealth who ate his food with an unfortunate relish. He had long since passed from the folly of Gastronomy into the sin of Gluttony. These two were the 'waverers'. Their minds had already been won over by her father's business acumen, but their hearts were not yet committed.

Much of the conversation, as always, bored Miss Ignatius that evening. It was about ships and tides and trade and the money that could be made, and the risks, of course, the risks. At one point Mr Sevigny attempted to tell an amusing story. He had been in the vineyards that afternoon instructing the labourers on a new planting, when he was confronted by a raging bull. 'The labourers, of course, all fled at the sight of the beast. They had more sense than I, perhaps, but if I were to flee as well you can imagine the talk that would have gone around. So I stood there with the bull perhaps twenty yards off. Its horns were massive and pointed in my direction.'

Lord Eccles interrupted, 'Was it pawing the ground and snorting steam from its nostrils?' His tongue slipped over his thick full lips as he spoke.

Mr Sevigny grew flustered. 'I cannot recollect. All my attention was upon its horns.'

'It's what they usually do before they charge. They stamp their hoof upon the ground and clouds of steam erupt from their nostrils. There is nothing more dangerous than a charging bull is there, Mr Sevigny?' Lord Eccles poured himself another drink and quaffed half of it.

'No, there is not. Unless you pull a red handkerchief out of your pocket and wave it at *El Toro*, which I did.'

'Which you did? A red flag to a bull? You are mad, sir. And then it did charge?' Lord Eccles raised his glass once more.

Mr Sevigny smiled. 'It did not charge. It walked towards me calmly, sniffing the air. It came up close to me and nuzzled me with its lovely wet nose. Such a charming bull, I thought, but you see that was the joke of it. It was not a bull at all. It was a cow. A gentle old cow, but still I did not know it at the time.'

'It is a splendid and delightful story,' Miss Ignatius said, although her hand fluttered up to her face when her smile threatened to become a yawn.

'A cow you say, Mr Sevigny?' Lord Eccles chuckled. 'I was confronted by a man-eating tiger once. I had his balls for breakfast. A most tasty dish it was, and said to increase a man's virility. Which it does. I am the living proof.'

Later, when the gentlemen retired to the smoking room, Lord Eccles manoeuvred Mr Sevigny into a corner. 'I've often wondered what it would be like to conjoin with a cow. Do you need a stool? Or a step-ladder? I imagine you would.'

Mr Sevigny pulled his shoulders back, pushed his chin into the air. 'Such a disgusting thought has never entered my mind.'

Lord Eccles sniffed. There was a wicked gleam in his eye. 'Really?' He reached down and in a flash had plucked a hair from Mr Sevigny's trouser leg. He held it up triumphantly. 'Hair of a cow, I do believe. Did you not change your clothes before coming to dinner?'

'I was in a rush, of course. The bull delayed me.'

'Cow,' Lord Eccles said.

At the moment that exchange was taking place Cassandra was removing her evening dress, her rigid corset, and pantaloons. She slipped into a simple white sleeping smock, unadorned except for a pretty string of pink roses embroidered around the neckline. Before her mirror, she undid her hair, the huge dark mass of it, and brushed it slowly, careful not to catch the eye of her reflection, and the questions it might ask. Then taking the razor, bowl and brush from her dresser, she hitched up her smock and soaped herself well. Firstly she removed the stubbly hairs from her legs and underarms then, with so much more care, she commenced to shave between her legs. She had been told by her mother once that the only flaw in her beauty was that she had too much body hair for a woman, so now she removed it all. The men she had lain with seemed to like it that way; more than one had said it helped with their arousal even when steeped in their cups.

No sooner had she finished her toilet than there was a knock at her door. 'Enter,' she said, hoping when it opened it would be the young one first, but it was not.

Lord Eccles swaggered into the room with a silver drinking flask in his hand, its sheen reflecting the candlelight in small glittering arcs. 'They tell me, my dear, that you are a pleasure in bed. They tell me I'm a pleasure in bed as well, so we shall make a pretty party of it, shan't we?'

Later, as Lord Eccles possessed her from behind, an image of Dr Travidian came unbidden into her mind. A sudden sense of shame swelled within her heart. Dr Travidian, such a strange man, the way his philosopher eyes had looked at her, not undressing her body as other men would, but as if they were reaching into her soul. Then he had taken her hand and kissed it, or had she offered it? She could not remember, but she had felt a sudden warmth run up her arm as if he had breathed some strange fire into her. She had been forced to turn away and pull her hand free, the night had been so hot and humid… But before she could capture that final thought, Lord Eccles whacked her on the buttocks in the glory of his spending, as if she were a favourite mare he'd taken for a trot around the park.

* * *

The next morning, over a breakfast of pumpernickel and poached eggs, Master Alexander Ignatius was discussing Dr Travidian's book—*The Seven Follies*—with his sister. Their father had a ship coming in on the early tide and had taken the ferry down the river to the port just after sunrise.

'Trumpery is another folly. Being overly fond of pretty and superficial things.' He cut into his egg and watched the yellow yolk soak into the coarse-grained bread.

Cassandra swatted a fly from her face and silently cursed the humidity. Another hot day without any rain, she was sure of it. The two waverers had now intellectually and emotionally committed their support to the expedition. Her father had kissed her and waved their cheques gleefully as he rushed out the door to catch the ferry. 'Rest today, dear child, rest,' he had said. 'Your work is done. The waverers are with us, and the doubters are no longer needed.'

Alexander knew nothing of this, but he did notice how tired his sister was, and therein saw an opportunity.

'And how does one tell if something is pretty but not superficial?' Cassandra asked.

Alexander thought for a moment, his forehead wrinkling. 'A flower,' he said, 'is pretty, but not superficial, for its prettiness serves a purpose in nature. Whereas the cheap jewellery of harlots is entirely superficial. It is pretty for the sake of being pretty.'

Cassandra felt a pang in her heart. 'I think a boy of your age would know little of harlots and their ways. Cheap jewellery, I am sure, is all they can afford. Perhaps all jewellery is Trumpery, even that made of gold, diamonds, sapphires, rubies and emeralds, or does their wealth make them more substantial?'

'I'm sure it does,' Alexander said, 'but I will need to study the matter further.' He stuffed the last piece of egg-soaked pumpernickel into his mouth, and excused himself to read more of Dr Travidian's book before it was time to leave for school.

Cassandra cried after him: 'And if the answer is not in his book, ask Dr Travidian whether all jewellery is Trumpery. I would be most interested to hear his answer.'

The only response from her brother was the thumping of his feet upon the stairs.

Cassandra twisted in her chair. Her father would bring her some Trumpery when he returned from the port. A string of pearls or another silk frock. He would kiss her on the forehead and tell her she was such a good daughter, and she would smile and thank him, as if it would help to hide the way she felt.

Upstairs, Master Alexander Ignatius crept into his sister's room. He locked the door behind him and approached the bed. There, he drew the sweat-stained sheets back and, with the tweezers he had taken from his sister's dresser, set about his task.

Part III: When Lovers Meet

Dr Travidian found Master Alexander's challenge completed when he returned to his rooms during the recess. For a moment, he stood staring at the pale green envelope that had been slipped beneath the door. Up to now, it had all been romantic fancy, but if he were to pick the envelope up, he would cross the line from fancy into folly. Yet pick it up he did, and a quick glance inside was enough to assure him the boy had done the deed.

From his desk drawer, Travidian took the Senora's powder, and placed one envelope inside the other. To the fireplace he went, struck a match with a nervous hand, ignited his folly and tossed it into the grate. The flame danced across the surface of the papery skin, then finding the spell's ingredients, with a sudden and dramatic puff, it flared. A purple bloom burst into existence, a wonderful fiery flower, then it was gone, and nothing but flat grey ashes remained.

* * *

Three days later, on a bleak Friday that oppressed the city with dark listless clouds, the porter brought Dr Travidian a letter from Lord Eccles.

'Dear Dr,' it read, 'I have recently become acquainted with your book on Joseph Hilarious and wish to meet with you to discuss our common interests in the work of this remarkable philosopher. His writings interest me greatly, as your own commentary on his work does. If you would be gracious enough to accept my invitation to dine this evening, I shall meet you at the Bull and Beaver at seven o'clock. I have heard tell it serves a passable venison stew and the ale is the most pleasant on the two sides of the river.

Yours affectionately,
Salawicious Eccles'

The letter puzzled Dr Travidian. His book on Joseph Hilarious was but a minor work written primarily for his pupils. Still, it would be inappropriate to decline the invitation of a wealthy businessman from such an old family. He took up his pen, wrote his acceptance, then rang for the porter.

With the students on the sports field, Travidian had intended to mark the pile of homework books that had sat neglected on his desk for most of the week. But a sudden restlessness had overcome him. Three days it was since he cast the spell. Three days too long. He had been a fool to think anything would come of it. Superstition was the folly that he was guilty of. Yet in such a state he could not get down to work. He took up his linen jacket, placed a straw hat upon his head and left for a stroll along the river.

Out the school gates and down the hill he went, until half-an-hour later he'd crossed St Lucia's bridge, where the idol of the martyred saint bestowed a knowing look with her famous cross-eyed gaze. Into the wealthier suburbs his feet took him where wide avenues and rows of poinciana trees with vermilion flowers spread out before him. Before too long he realised he was almost at the Ignatius residence.

Travidian would, he decided, knock upon the door, give the maid his calling card and hope to be received. But when he reached the gate, he walked past it, up to the end of the street and crossed to the other side.

He must go to the door, he told himself, knock upon it... perhaps if she were to see him with her own eyes the spell would wake and its magic set in motion.

Miss Ignatius was sitting upon the upstairs verandah, reading *The Seven Follies* that she had taken from her brother's room. She had just about decided that Joseph Hilarious would have declared all jewellery to be Trumpery when she happened to glance down into the street. There was no mistaking the figure of the gentleman who walked so nonchalantly along. Her heart gave an unexpected flutter. Would he call? Should she wave to him, call out... She stood and placed her hands on the filigree railing of the verandah and looked into the sky as if studying a bird flying by.

By contrast, Dr Travidian was studying his feet, counting each step he took, knowing that soon he must decide or walk by once more, cross the bridge and return to his dreary rooms. A moment later, he was opening the old iron gate of the Ignatius house, feeling light-headed, climbing the sandstone steps, and before he had even thought of what he would say he had knocked upon the door.

Miss Ignatius left the verandah, and raced down the stairs. She shooed the maid aside, and took several deep breaths as she walked down the hall. She saw him through the door's leadlights. Tall, straight, so formally standing there. He would look into her eyes... if she let him... reach into her soul. She put a blank mask on her face. 'Dr Travidian,' she said, when finally that door was opened, 'I presume you've come to talk about Alexander. I do hope his behaviour has improved.'

* * *

Dr Travidian returned from Miss Ignatius's house in a fine and jolly mood. Certainly, they had done little more than exchange the usual pleasantries before they had both become lost for words—it would rain, perhaps it would not, it was exceedingly humid, et cetera—but there had been a warmth in Miss Ignatius's manner and demeanour, which he had not encountered before. He now had an invitation to afternoon tea on Sunday, ostensibly to further discuss Alexander's progress at school, but it was a start. Yes, a most wonderful start, Travidian thought. Perhaps it was in such subtle ways the Senora's magic worked.

Shortly before he was due to meet Lord Eccles, Travidian went to his window to check the weather. It had looked like a thunderstorm was brewing earlier, but now the clouds hung as listlessly as ever. Down in the quadrangle, a tall gentleman was standing, his dark clothes blurring his figure in the twilight. He appeared to be looking up at Travidian's window. It was long past the time for the day-boys to have departed, and the boarders would all be at supper, hungry and fatigued after a day of swinging the willow in the summer heat. And the figure was too slender for another of the teachers who were all older than Travidian and on the portly side. Now the man raised his hand as if to wave, but no… it could not be… he was blowing a kiss.

Dr Travidian drew away from the window, and pulled the curtains shut. What nonsense. Surely, he was mistaken. He checked his watch. It was time he was off to dine with Lord Eccles. But when he entered the quadrangle, he found the man still there, and walking rapidly in his direction.

'May I be of assistance?' Travidian asked when their paths met.

'Dr Travidian,' the other said, 'I am so very pleased to meet you. So very pleased… but, where are my manners… please allow me to introduce myself. Francis Sevigny, at your service, dear doctor.'

Travidan looked closely at the figure before him. The man's cheeks were flushed a rosy pink. He smelt of sweat and some exotic scent. Had this gentleman really blown him a kiss? 'And what is it I may do for you, Mr Sevigny?'

'Francis, please.' Sevigny shifted awkwardly. 'Please call me Francis.'

'Mr Sevigny, I prefer not to address people I have just met, and do not know, by their Christian names. Now if you would be so kind as to tell me what your business is.'

Mr Sevigny cringed on hearing those words. 'Please, doctor, I beg of you, don't make this more difficult than it already is.'

Dr Travidian took a handkerchief from his pocket and wiped his brow. Damn the heat. Where was the rain? 'More difficult than what is?'

'I think you know what I'm talking about, David.'

'I understand nothing of what you are saying, Mr Sevigny. Now if you will excuse me I have an urgent appointment.' But before he could move off, Sevigny reached out and grasped his arm.

'David, my dear fellow, I'm sure this is as big a shock to you as it is to me, but really there is no need to be rude.'

Travidian shook himself free. A look of fragile despair passed across Sevigny's face. His hand crept into his pocket and emerged bearing a crumpled rose bloom. 'I brought this for you.'

Travidian took a step backwards. He was now convinced the poor man was suffering some illness of the mind. 'Mr Sevigny, it is a lovely flower,' he said by way of appeasement.

'Its fragrance is exceptional.'

'I have no doubt,' Travidian replied, 'but as pretty as it is, I am afraid that I really do have an appointment to keep.' He strode away, but heard the footsteps of the other man close behind.

'You should not treat me like this,' Sevigny cried. 'I would deny my love for you if I could, but I cannot, and I do not believe you wish me to. I know in my heart you feel the same as I do.'

Dr Travidian quickened his pace, then began to run, dashing through the school gates and up the hill to the Bull and Beaver. But he was more used to sitting at a desk than fleeing danger. The wild-eyed Mr Sevigny caught him at the door to the tavern, leaping upon him and attempting to wrestle him to the ground.

'I know where you were this afternoon. I followed you. You think the Ignatius whore will make you happy, when mine is the only love you shall ever need.'

Travidian jabbed his elbow into Sevigny's ribs, and fled along the cobbled street headlong into a handsome cab coming from the other direction. He jumped away, but lost his footing, heard the frightened whinny of a horse, and the clashing of its hooves, as his forehead struck the gutter.

When next he knew what was happening he found himself lying on a seat inside the handsome cab. Through dizzy eyes, he saw a round florid face staring down at him. The man licked his lips and said, 'Dr Travidian? Lord Eccles at your service. Good God, to think I almost killed you. I would never have forgiven myself. Never in a million years, dear boy.'

Lord Eccles placed an open flask against Travidian's lips. 'Here drink this. It will do you the world of good.'

Travidian spluttered as the fiery taste of it hit his tongue.

'Absinthe,' Lord Eccles said. 'It's wonderful to write poetry by. The drink of the true romantic, which I admit freely I am not. Just a simple businessman who has a lust for life.'

Travidian eased himself up. 'I was fleeing a madman. He declared his love for me.'

'A profane love, is it? Why, what a scandalous man! Tell me his name. I shall challenge him to a duel, if you wish, to protect your good name. Pistols at dawn, or rapiers, if you prefer. I'm a good shot—killed a tiger once, ate his balls for breakfast—and I'm a fine hand with a rapier too.'

Lord Eccles handed him his flask once more. Travidian took a long swig this time. The pounding in his head was easing to a gentler rhythm, but when he next looked across the compartment he saw that Lord Eccles's fly was unbuttoned to reveal a cockstand of generous proportion.

'It is rather magnificent, don't you think? It was the tiger balls that did the trick.' The silly smile upon Lord Eccles' face was that of a naughty boy who was delighted at being caught with his pants down.

Travidian groaned. Surely, he had fallen asleep upon his desk whilst marking the student's books, and would awaken soon. He lunged for the door, grabbed the handle, and flung himself from the moving cab. Then he was rolling and bouncing, on the cobbles again, rolling down that hill he'd climbed such a short while ago.

Part IV: Love Follies

Concussed, his body bruised and aching, feeling altogether as if he had just crawled from his grave, Travidian found his way back to his rooms to find the nightmare was not yet over.

The lovelorn Mr Sevigny was sitting at Travidian's desk, a little silver pistol with a pearl handle cocked in his hand. 'I love you, yet you spurn my love. What have I done that you should treat me so?'

'Mr Sevigny, I beseech you…'

'Francis. You must call me Francis.' Sevigny waved his gun.

Travidian swallowed hard. His head was playing the tattoo of a military band: bagpipes, drums and fifes were ringing in his ears. 'Francis, please, I beseech you to put down your weapon.'

'So dearly do I love you I would kill you, and myself, rather than have you to lose your heart to that Ignatius whore. And a whore she most assuredly is. Why I myself bed her but four nights ago after Lord Eccles had already stirred his porridge in her pot. She whores for her father, to seal his business deals. Yet she takes to it with such a relish that is at once both fiendish and delightful.'

Travidian wished he were deaf in that moment. It was all lies, nothing but the jealous raving of a madman, but yet… three hairs… three hairs of others who had been in her bed? His head swam. 'It is a monstrous lie, you disgusting wretch!'

Sevigny's face grew pale. A tear dropped from the corner of his eye. The gun shook in his hand, but then came a loud thumping outside. In the next instant, there was a thunderous crash upon the door and Lord Eccles burst into the room.

'Dear boy,' he cried, 'I came to most humbly apologise for my behaviour earlier this evening.' From the corner of his eye he caught Sevigny with his gun and turned upon him. 'What in the name of all the furies of hell is a miserable cow-poking son of a wine-maker doing in the good doctor's rooms? And with a gun? Answer me, you insolent cur. I demand it.'

'He is the madman I told you about,' Travidian said, and thought, 'and you are another.'

'I love him with all the passion of my heart,' Sevigny said, 'but he loves another.'

'Damn you, Sevigny! Of course, he loves another.' Lord Eccles roared, bellowing with all the force of his lungs.

'More fool you. It is the Ignatius whore he loves. Not you or I.'

'She is not a whore,' Travidian protested; she could not be. He would not believe it.

'Tell him, my lord, tell him what you did with her but four nights ago. Lift the veil of love from his ungrateful eyes.'

Lord Eccles turned to Travidian, saw the look of abject hopelessness on his face. His heart went out to him. 'Poor fellow,' he thought, 'I do love him so, and if I do love him so…' For a moment he felt the power of those tiger balls swell up within him, giving him a nobility hitherto unknown in his life of lusty Trumpery. It was a most wonderful feeling. 'Miss Cassandra Ignatius is a most lovely lady and a most loyal daughter who brings nothing but honour to her family. Whereas you, Mr Sevigny, are a cheap and nasty liar. Cheap and nasty like the wines your family makes. If you as so much touch a hair on this lovely man's head, I shall smash your skull in.' He pulled his absinthe flask from his pocket and raised it high.

'I will shoot you first,' Sevigny cried. His cheeks were again alive with passion. 'How dare you insult the good name of my family.'

'Shoot me, will you!' Lord Eccles stammered. 'With that pipsqueak pistol. It shall leave but a graze on my skin. I have a hide of leather.'

It was in that moment that the full laughing face of his folly reared up before Dr Travidian. If it was not a dream, not a nightmare, then it was simply sheer living absurdity. Two grown men, at once prominent and respectable in their own right, arguing over his love! The folly was his alone no longer.

A mournful bellow rose up from the quadrangle below.

Sevigny who appeared to be at his wits end shook with the sound of it. His face was ghastly pale again and his hair, slick with sweat, clung to his head, looking as if some slimy sea creature had taken up residence there.

Lord Eccles saw his chance. The flask flew from his hand, straight and fast. It found its mark, sending the gun flying from Sevigny's hand.

Another bellow sounded below.

'Ah, ha! A shot, sir, a veritable shot it was.' Lord Eccles puffed himself up like a peacock.

'My wrist, my wrist! Damn you, you have broken my wrist, you drunken demon.'

Travidian rushed to the window. Down below, the large dark eyes of a long-horned cow looked up at him. She bellowed once more when she saw his face.

'Hear that,' Lord Eccles said. 'It is the love song of the domestic bovine. I do believe it is *El Toro*. Your girlfriend has come looking for you, Sevigny.'

Travidian turned from the window. 'I beseech you, gentlemen, that if you love me as you say you do, then to demonstrate your love to me, you must first make peace and love each other.' And with that he was gone, rushing from the room and down the stairs, almost knocking over the porter in his flight.

'Wake the watchman from his bed,' he called as he passed. 'There are two madmen in my room who are intent on killing each other. It would be best if we saved both their lives.'

'And there is a mad old cow in the quadrangle,' the porter replied, 'mooing at your window.'

'Don't worry,' Travidian said, taking the stairs two at a time, 'I shall charm her.'

The cow mooed sweetly when she saw him, tossed her horns and went to him. He gave her his hand and let her sniff it. She nuzzled it and licked his fingers with her thick curly tongue. 'You are a beautiful creature,' he said, throwing his coat over her and climbing upon her back. 'Now away to my beloved, my pretty cow.'

Travidian grasped the hump upon her back as they went, across the quadrangle and out the school gates at a fast trot and then slowly up the hill, past the Bull and Beaver, and then down the other side and to the river's edge where stood the less than salubrious Chicken Whistle. Here the painted whores, sailors and the wharfies, came tumbling out the doors as Travidian and his cow came riding by. And such a sight it was, they clapped their hands, and laughed and begged him to tarry for while. Surely, there was a story to be told.

And Travidian, with absinthe reigning in his veins, and folly ruling his heart, was happy to oblige. 'Who will bring me a tankard of beer, and some forage for my loyal cow?'

The cow was fed, the beer was brought and a stool for him to sit upon. 'There are two who profess their love for me,' Travidian began. 'This cow, she loves me too. But silly clown I am, I love another. It started with a folly. Love-forlorness…'

'Love makes fools of us all,' someone cried out.

'But then the true folly began with a spell created by a witch…' And so he told them the tale, and when he had finished, the publican of the Chicken Whistle came and placed a jester's cap his head. It was of red and green velvet and held a brass bell on each of its three peaks.

'Every fool needs a cap,' the publican said, 'and I am told this here one is the same sort as worn by Hilarious the Clown when he juggled on the corner of Pit and Bank all those years ago.'

Travidian shook his head. The bells jingled merrily. If it was good enough for the Clown it was good enough for him. He climbed back upon his cow and rolled along the street once more. 'Farewell, my friends, farewell.'

Down to the river and across the bridge he went, passing into the broad avenues until the Ignatius house rose up before him with its pretty verandah and bright lights.

How nervous he had been earlier that day. How silly and foolish and brave he felt now. He climbed down from his cow, tethered her to the iron fence, pushed through the gate, and walked up the sandstone steps on wobbly legs. He knocked upon the door. The nightmare had turned into a fabulous dream, and he no longer cared if he were awake or asleep.

When the door opened, Cassandra Ignatius was there. Travidian, in the grip of absurdity, jingled the bells upon his hat and danced a little jig up and down the steps. The look on Cassandra Ignatius's face was unfathomable. Travidian stopped dancing. He looked into the dark grey depths of her eyes. 'I'm a clown,' he said, 'and a drunken one at that.' He bowed clumsily. 'I came to tell you that I love…' but then he staggered, was about to fall.

A smile quivered at the corner of Cassandra Ignatius's mouth as she rushed to his side, and when she took his arm she trembled as she did so.

The Author: Geoffrey Maloney

Geoffrey Maloney lives in Brisbane. His story '5 Cigarettes and 2 Snakes' appeared in *Aurealis #1*. Geoffrey's most recent short stories have appeared in *Beneath Ceaseless Skies*, but most of his writing of late has been dedicated to the novel *Legends of the Black Flag*, which is set in British India in the 1870s.

Story Behind the Story

Vaguely, at the heart of 'The Bewitching of Dr Travidian' lies an old English folktale that I read about a long time ago. At the same time I've spent the last few years reading a great deal of late Victorian era literature including novels, travel memoirs and histories. This was by way of background research for the long novel I have been working on set in British India. But as an avid reader I found myself quickly becoming addicted to the literary genre known as the Victorian sensational novel. Such novels were rich in language and plot, somewhat scandalous in their subject matter, laced with melodrama, and at times delved into the supernatural. Dr Travidian is my own humorous pastiche of this delightful and historic genre.

The Illustrator: Peter Allert

Peter Allert illustrated his first children's book in 2011 called *Long Live Us*, written by Edel Wignell and published by IP Kids. He is a member of the Brisbane Illustrators Group (BIG) and creates detailed watercolour illustrations of photographs he has taken around Asia. Peter has exhibited his work in the Brisbane Square Library and other locations around Brisbane. More of his work can be seen on his website peterallert.com.au and on the BIG website brisbaneillustrators.com.

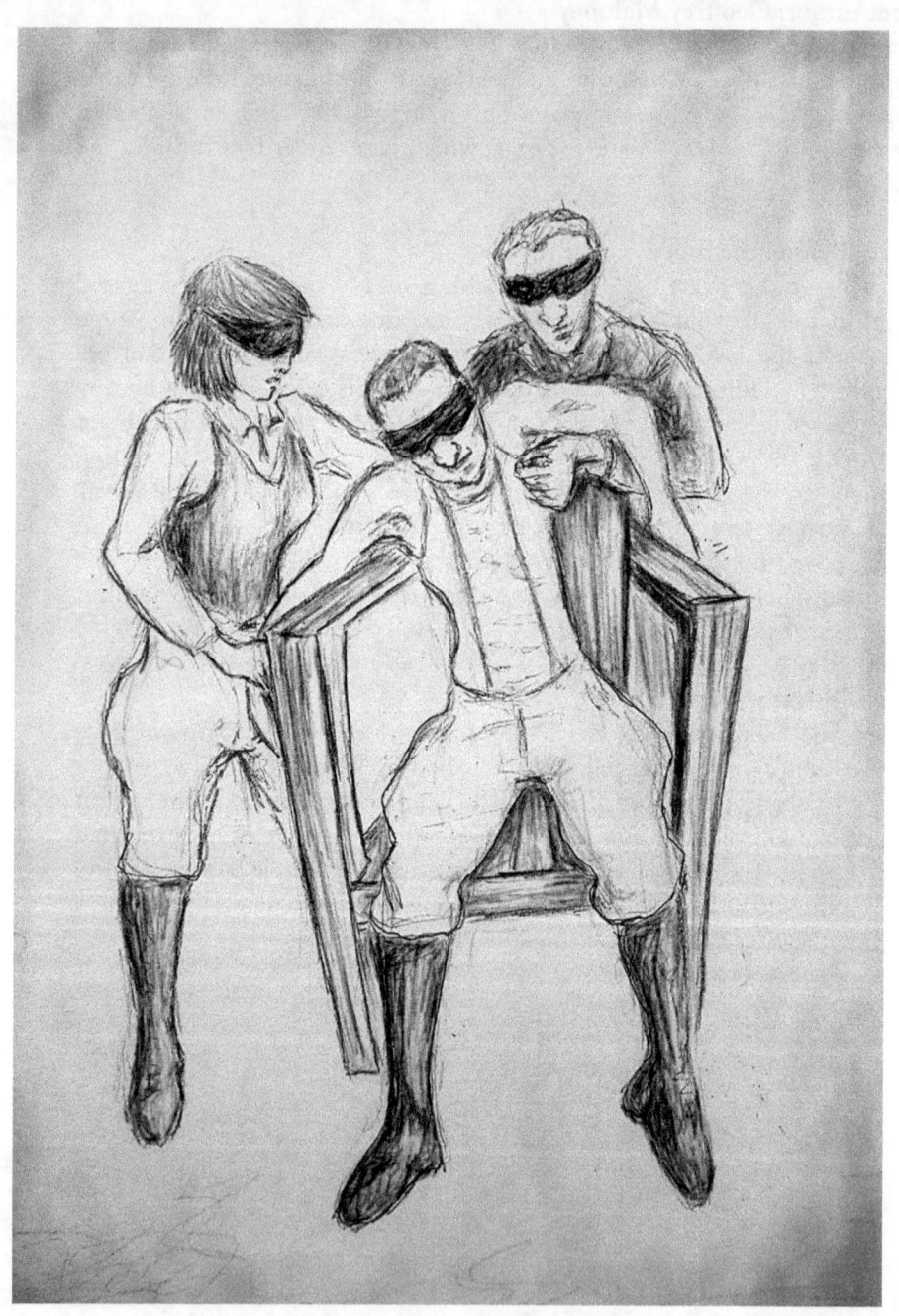

Illustration by Kate Harrison

The Madlock Chair

Terry Dowling

They had been eighteen leaving the Baylieu Gate, fourteen by the centre of the Gadarene Spread, twelve at Quitmus, nine by the outer precincts of the Indra Circle, but seven, only seven, when they reached The Madlock itself.

On a good day, Sam Aitchander might have foreseen such a terrible loss of life. So many alien Landings scattered across the Earth, manifestations from elsewhere like the name said, many of them here in the burning heart of Australia, and the four close by The Madlock were among the worst of them.

Sagueiro's people had modelled the outcomes at the highest levels, had believed they'd known what to expect. But *eleven* dead! It had been Sam's call leaving their armoured ATVs at Quitmus and doing the final leg on foot, his call going past The Sidewinder like that. He took it hard.

'Is it there?' Sagueiro asked, oblivious, pretend oblivious, who could say, a stark minatory shape in his Rockfall crisis suit. The pre-noon glare was terrible. Even with tek-spec shades you couldn't be absolutely sure what you were getting.

Sam wore his usual flashman kit: retro whipcord breeches, long faux-skin duster, field pack. He raised the intensity on his spec-set. 'It will be. Active phase, the average is five times a day.'

The Madlock sat on the red desert like the promise of a great house, a small town: a pedestal base at least two hectares square—a vast stone-like table a metre high reached by four steps 'carved' out of the eastern side.

Sometimes a doorframe appeared atop those steps, just like any pre-fab doorframe on any human house, smooth, metallic-looking, as if giving official access to the flat windy space. Sometimes the frame appeared elsewhere on the site, and not just at the edges, suggesting access to interior domains. A door out on The Madlock deck suggested interiors the way a window frame suggested views.

And sometimes a tiny roil sat in that door-field where a lock or handle might have been on any door you could trust, giving the site its name. The lock-point twisted and danced and held, sometimes for hours, then fell away to nothing. Then the frame vanished too until the next active phase, days, weeks, seasons later.

Sagueiro moved nearer, brought his compressed, near-noon shadow closer to Sam's, though not letting them touch. He knew the flashman's reputation, and people in Sam's life had just died. 'Mr Aitch, I meant what I said at the briefing in Melbourne. I don't pretend our thinking is new. But I do not automatically see these Landings as parts of an invasion. Landings is entirely the wrong name for them. I see them as breaches. Rupture points between worlds, quantum corridors. Not necessarily intentional or focused. The evidence supports it.'

'Just happening to manifest as deadly installations.' Sam truly wasn't in the mood.

'A shock reaction. These intrusions are overwhelmed by the sheer complexity—the alien-ness—of what *they* encounter. They respond, adapt as best they can, desperately try to manage. Defend themselves. But random, I suspect. Trying to render bits of the psychic storm.'

'The Horse, The Blue Ship, The Old Angel. Quite a storm.'

'Rendered fragments of ideation is all, just like The Madlock here.'

Sam looked out across the windswept deck. 'We're full circle then, like you say. Wild compensation was Jarrett's claim.'

'And he died trying to prove it. But we think he was on to something. The Landings are highly reactive, but not necessarily self-directing. Old theory, maybe, but still sound, still needing consideration. Trends and fashion can't rule this.'

Sam turned back to Sagueiro. He'd expected this overture. 'But you *do* still allow alien life? Actual lifeforms?'

'That's easy. But we step back from that too. They *present* like that is all we're saying. We allow the full range—viruses, machines, programs, probes, alien organics, rogue quantum artefacts, the lot. We won't push preferences.'

Sam kept his voice even. Maybe Sagueiro did deserve better. 'You gave it straight in Melbourne then. You're here to do exactly what you said. Communicate.'

'So cynical, Mr Aitch. Is it so improbable?'

We've lost lives, Sam might have said, *if* words were needed. The Landings had been quiet, down-phased. Suddenly they'd gone active all the way from Baylieu. Caught them without a prime flash crew, the rest of his team out on contract, as you did in down-phase, as he was doing with Sagueiro's team now.

Saw us coming!

No need to say that either. It had already damaged enough of this newly dangerous day. As for communication, being more moderate, more forbearing, he might have said it's been tried. Again and again, ad infinitum. But the truth was it should be tried. Always. Constantly. But lives! Sadjin with his jokes. Polly Tomay with her newest shoulder tatt. Regus. Tall price for one more attempt at a first-contact conversation.

But Sam felt the old yearning too. You couldn't keep coming out among the Landings and not have something of it. This was alien invasion on a global scale, or not. If so, where was the rest of it, the accelerating follow-through? If not, why not? 'You're seeing the sites themselves, all their hunt avatars—the whirter, burrus and ayling variants—everything, as acts of contact rather than predation.'

'Trauma response, Mr Aitch, like I said. Patches on wounds. Protection.'

'The old immune system argument.'

'But not even that. Not necessarily directed retaliation at all. Worlds break through. What form would those patches take? We allow everything. We'll use focused telepathy, tailored psionic bursts, to get past the retaliation cycles if we can, allow more than your usual coherent alien source, but rather an earnestly de-alienising source too—'

'Explain that.'

Sagueiro seized on the chance, actually lifted his shades away from his deep blue eyes, trying for goodwill, seeming to. But only seven left now. They really did need each other.

'Learning us. Stepping down from alien-ness to some kind of interface, even in spite of natural, even preferred, responses. Just as we've been trying to do for decades. Need to keep doing.'

'It's still being tried at a global level.'

'At a token level, Mr Aitch. The headlines keep giving the damage stats. Hard to compete with what looks like culling.'

'Hard to argue otherwise when the Landings reach out and murder millions.'

'Kill, not necessarily murder.'

'Right,' Sam begrudged it. Who knew why the Landings reached out as they did, sent a hundred thousand into catatonic shutdown here, fifty thousand there, did it again and again for decades now. But Sagueiro was absolutely correct. Ways of thinking, seeing, the old habits, were the *real* enemy here.

Sagueiro sensed the new opportunity. 'You flashmen showed us the way, kept going out among the Landings, stopped them sending these messages of death.'

'Sometimes.'

'Sometimes. But you continue to do it. You developed the skills needed to make them switch modes and save many of those lives. You haven't given up. You need to accept that we've groomed a new skill set is all. We need to try it out by coming here.'

'And pre-tested how? You didn't disclose that in Melbourne.'

Sagueiro ignored the comment, nodded towards The Madlock. 'We're confident, Mr Aitch.' *Need to know.*

'I accepted clearance level exclusiveness on this, Sagueiro, but eleven down, I'm asking direct. Pre-tested how?'

'Blacky Varrac took us to The Quintain. We did our tests. It stayed dormant.'

Sam let it pass. The Quintain and tests. Just another way of saying need to know. Then belatedly grasped the implication. *Had no losses.* Not arrogance or stubbornness then. Consideration in view of what had happened over the past two days, the whirters reaching out like that, actually snatching them out of the vehicles, taking some, leaving others, as if choosing from a menu.

'And The Madlock?'

'What I said on Tuesday. It still tracks as the most non-lethal Landing in Australia. Highest energy readings. In the middle of some of the worst, I know, but—'

'The Blue Ship, The Night Tree. The Sidewinder. You might say that.'

'—no logged hunt avatars that we know of, no remotes, no overt aggression components. You know the profile. You help maintain the database.'

'Your people will have modelled the possibility that those Landings may *be* its avatars. They're geographically very close.'

'We do allow that. Of course we do. A host CPU like The Caress. But it's below nine percent. The available data—global data—suggests we're safe here. In a still point at least.'

Sam surveyed the blazing, wind-swept deck of The Madlock again. Eleven lives to get here: a line of reprisal all the way from Baylieu. A long way from random right there. So much for still points and safety.

* * *

At 1400 the doorframe cycled in and took its classic position atop the steps, the 'lock' roiling a handspan in from the upper right edge.

Sagueiro had his team ready. He crossed to his four primaries, the two women and two men painstakingly trained for this one task, and had them make a classic diamond wand formation. Then, just like deploying an actual flash crew on any other day, Sagueiro sent them forward to the foot of the steps.

Sam's remaining scout, the tall Ethiopian, Assicante, did a slow circuit of the perimeter, keeping watch. She'd lost Polly and Regus in the last sixteen hours and was doubtless in that place that too much loss took you to, a lean guarded shape as she moved along, now and then pausing to watch, like a child's drawing of a resting eagle.

It was all still-life and dumb-show then, the sun a fiery coin in the white haze, the four unmoving shapes at the roil, Sagueiro to the side, Assicante stationary on a dune ridge now, and himself standing back, one moment watching The Madlock expanse, the next scanning the distances.

Psionic bursts were probing that roil-point, courting it, grooming it, urging it to declare, no doubt providing the appropriate human semantic counters, perhaps achieving little more than the fact of controlled stimulus coming in, further trauma risk, further cause for reprisal, perhaps not even that. But shape, form and intent anyway, something, and again a long way from random.

Nothing random here, Sam decided, certain of it, and with eleven out of eighteen lost like that, most not even in trail-side graves, he kept seeing only death and reprisal, simple truth.

* * *

At 1442 an artefact appeared out on the deck, modest, indistinct, just a juddering fleck in the expanse.

Specs locked and gave it in seconds, though you allowed for eye-brain tampering and automatically photo verified, cross-confirmed. Assicante came in from her circuit to exchange two words.

'A chair.'

'A chair.'

A chair-form at least, and nowhere near as sketch-book minimal as the doorframe and steps. Through the shimmer, the glare, the endless fluxes and force eddies coursing over the site, it looked retro, tooled, even handcrafted, as if, yet again, to meet a template sought, tracked and plucked from a human mind.

It was terrifying in its ordinariness. Like The Horse with its lines of antique horse-forms arrayed across the spinifex dunes at Cantra, The Station Master with its click-clicking line switches and vintage railway semaphores endlessly signalling on the gibber flats at Parlier, this was profound, insistent, devastating in its implications. Invasion, interface or patches on wounds, this single manifestation teased, taunted, haunted the human mind, denying random.

Sagueiro's team didn't break off. They were spec-sighted. *If* using eyes at all, they would certainly know the artefact was there.

But Sagueiro beckoned Sam and Assicante over, surveillance be damned, raised his shades again, eye-claim courtesy in the old way.

'We go to it. The team keeps sending.'

'Surveillance?' Sam asked, protocol rather than preference.

Sagueiro shrugged. 'Trade off. I need to be out there. Assicante can stay.'

'We're down to seven and I'm responsible,' Sam said. 'I stay.'

Sagueiro nodded and moved to the steps; Assicante followed. They climbed to the deck, started off into the shimmer, the wind and fluxes kicking the tails of Assicante's duster into banners.

What else was happening? Sam wondered, fighting for whatever overview he could manage. This was the most non-lethal, least dangerous Landing in

Australia, one of the least dangerous in the world, but configurations had changed, the sites had gone active. For all he knew The Madlock was even now reaching out across the planet, sending countless thousands into catatonic fugue to die from exposure and neglect before aid could reach them. Two figures becoming lost in the shimmer out there and worlds could be ending.

With no flash crew!

Surveillance be damned!

Sam headed for the steps. If The Madlock turned, summoned, if avatars did come hunting, so be it. He climbed to the deck, started after the others.

They weren't surprised to see him when he joined them at the chair. No-one commented, certainly not Sam, though Assicante immediately headed back to resume her perimeter. What you did. Protocol not preference.

Sam had choices. He could cancel the mission, insist they withdraw altogether, but other than that, site decisions were Sagueiro's now, and he was using his throat link to send data back to his team, all triple repeats to offset the flux distortions. When the soft murmuring ceased, Sam asked the obvious. 'Will you sit in it?'

'Of course.'

'What are your people getting?'

'The energies have cycled up.'

'We should wait. See if it's a recurring feature.'

'I know. But what if it's an overture? A one-time invitation?'

'Sagueiro, the sites have turned. This could be an avatar as deadly as an ayling or a whirter, and you're an irreplaceable resource here. Without you, the mission ends.'

'Gillian can continue with the others.'

'Probably not.' *I can shut this down.* 'Send a volunteer.'

'The first change on record for this site,' Sagueiro said. 'Nothing may happen.' *We have no volunteers.*

'Angler fish, Sagueiro. You know the drill. This could be the lure.'

'Mr Aitch—Sam—I need to do this. *You* need me to.' Bold. Bold. 'We've sacrificed a lot to get here.'

They had different lives, in some ways lives as alienised from each other as from the Landing itself. But again Sagueiro was right. There was only this.

Sam stepped back three paces. Sagueiro nodded, murmured further instructions, then moved to the chair.

'Get them out if you can,' he said.

Then sat.

And vanished, chair and all. The spec readings went wild, peaked, settled.

Barely thirty seconds and Assicante was on the link. 'He's here on a dune,

Sam. Dead but otherwise intact. No obvious injuries. No sign of the chair.'

'I'm coming in.'

* * *

Gillian Saimo and Glynnis Faimin had the body bagged but still unzipped. After all, how dead was dead out here? How Sagueiro was Sagueiro, for that matter? If chairs and doorframes, horses and antique railway signals then why not the faux corpses of mission commanders? Patches on wounds.

'What now?' Sam asked.

Gillian was competent, crisis-toughened, doing her best in spite of everything. 'We continue sending. Try for another response.' She didn't say chair—or one with Sagueiro in it. As with Polly and Regus, you sometimes discovered what the connections were at the end of things, love and lives suddenly asunder.

'And what, Gillian? *You* sit in it?' *Try for a trade?*

'Just working the site. Getting what we can.'

With *twelve* lives lost.

'Aye. Say how you want us then.'

'Thanks, Aitch.' No Mr now. Connection wherever she could make it.

The team reformed at the steps. Sam and Assicante stood watch again. The sun blazed, the wind sent eddies of sand hissing across the deck, guided, shaped and turned by unseen fluxes.

At 1551 the team began sending.

At 1558 another chair appeared—the same chair, a different one, who could say, and Assicante did escort duty once more as Gillian Saimo went to it.

Sam watched them go, again thinking of the other Landings close by, watching, waiting, being, considered their variety, the sheer otherness: The Blue Ship's great prow, The Sidewinder's curves, so much damascene steel tricked out as codes of light, snatching them up one by one, so casually, so matter-of-factly. His thoughts ranged even further beyond, out to the lines of horses in the afternoon light at Cantra, to The Station Master's signals and switches signing, shifting, to The Sailmaker's face-screens now taut, now bellying in the heated air. A chair was such a small thing by comparison, but you always allowed the small-big—always!—something vast and encompassing marked by the smallest edge.

'Gillian?' he asked.

'Identical,' she said, no repeats needed. The fluxes were down, the energy readings comparatively stable. 'All quiet here. I'm going to—'

'Gillian, wait! Do nothing!'

'What, Aitch? Sam, what is it?'

'Do nothing till I get there!'

And Sam reached them eight minutes later with Sagueiro's bagged corpse slung over his shoulder, carefully laid it down three metres from the chair. Assicante clearly wanted to stay, but she nodded once and went back to make a perimeter, again protocol not preference.

Gillian watched wide-eyed. 'You don't think…?'

'A hunch is all.'

'Aitch—?'

'We gave something new. It gave something new. We acted. It acted.'

'Stimulus response. Tropisms. Not necessarily directed. Not—'

'But what if they are? We have to allow that we're *teaching* it—something. *If* that's the case, what it did, what it gave, what it *learned* is unacceptable. We show it that. At the very least, Gillian, we show it that.'

She nodded, and together they worked Sagueiro's body out of the bag, not daring to acknowledge the new indignities and what had been lost, hauled it to the chair as if baggage, property, so much less. Together they let it slump back onto the seat.

Again chair and occupant vanished.

Again they waited for Assicante's call. Sam actually expected: 'He's here, Aitch!' at any moment. But when she did use the link, her news was far more pedestrian, even if more of a surprise somehow.

'The chair is here. Just the chair. The lock and frame have gone.'

'Confirm.'

'We have the chair. The lock has gone. The site has shut down.'

'No sign of Sagueiro?'

'Negative. Just the chair.'

'Start an analysis, Asa. We're coming in.'

* * *

The chair was as close to being chemically inert as the great majority of Landing material, giving the same narrow and limited band of readings as marked the doorframe, The Station Master's signal towers, the horse-forms at Cantra, the decorated balconies of The Spanish Lantern.

'We take it back with us,' Sam said, the only possible decision he could make under the circumstances, something that *could* be salvaged.

Then they made an overnight bivouac close enough to the steps but sufficiently clear of the maximum active-phase flux radius just in case, intending to set off for Baylieu at first light.

Sam could only hope that with The Madlock in down-phase, the other sites might be as well, but would make a wide detour back to the

ATVs just the same.

It was on Assicante's mind too, of course, and just before dawn she knelt by him to talk.

'Aitch, the sites went wildfire. Has to be years.'

'Your point, Asa?'

'Could be *us, this!*'

'They knew we were coming.'

'Exactly.' The implications were devastating, and Assicante spoke the worst. 'More than targeting. Conducting experiments too.' And more specific, even more alarming: 'Targeting flashmen *away* from their full flash crews. Getting back at us.'

Sam resisted it. These were *human* imperatives, *human* responses, *human* solutions. But what if? 'We have to make it back, Asa. Have to try.'

'Aye,' she said. 'But we have the chair. We put it out on the deck. I sit in it.'

'The site's shut down.'

'They were down-phase before the wildfire. Always active, I'm betting.'

'The risk, Asa.'

'There either way, I figure. Need to do something.'

Sam resisted that too, then relented as she'd known he would. After all, their eighteen were now six. Even with the ATVs, what were the chances? 'Aye. At first light then.'

* * *

It was surprising how mundane, how *unsurprising* it was when they set out the chair at 0610. The runs with Sagueiro—living and dead—suddenly seemed like rehearsals for this single simple act, as if this too had been planned all along.

Gillian and Sam stood by as Assicante set the chair in approximately the same position as on the previous day, nodded once and sat.

And vanished, chair and scout both.

There were no residues this time, none that were apparent at least, nothing out on the dunes or within range of their scanners. The site remained closed, fluxes flatlined.

They waited four hours, repeating tests, searching the distances. At 1020 they set off for Baylieu.

* * *

They were two hours along when the wildfire avatars came, first the whirters, a dozen of the fourteen-part death-ball vortices assembling before their eyes, reaching cohesion and rushing in, quick and deadly.

But before the forerunners could achieve kill-range, something wondrous happened: an equal number of Sagueiro manqués appeared as decoy defence, allowing themselves to be struck down, consumed, sending the whirters into spectacular disarray, leaving the neutralised cores to hang spinning in the air, summoning replacement parts, trying to rebuild.

As soon as they did so, each lethal dandelion haze springing forward, more Sagueiros were there, stiff-legged, clearly faux, and now with Assicantes scattered among them as well.

And the positioning—always an amplification of the classic diamond wand formation! It was. Every time. Sagueiros and Assicantes in *that* alignment, running, leaping, lunging forward from that classic configuration to break the pattern and shield Sam's people.

It knows what it's taken, he realised. Knows what it's trying to give back!

It's trying to create a flash crew!

Couldn't hope to, of course. How could it? But like a child copying its parents in the kitchen, in the garden, in the workshop, there were the broader strokes, possible intention.

Mimicry or communication, Sam didn't care. He led his team on, and with every Sagueiro or Assicante snatched out of the world, a replacement was there, so their eighteen—their *eighteen!*—never diminished.

When the burrus hunt-forms appeared, rushing fist-size balls of airborne porcelain, the Sagueiros and Assicantes were there again to sacrifice themselves, flinging themselves forward to take the strikes, their replacements always making the count of eighteen.

And when the aylings came running, human-form death-dolls leaping across the dunes to complete their fleschette detonations, there was—startlingly!—an altogether different defence response. A chair appeared in front of each running form and, by whatever sudden compulsion, the doll would turn, sit and vanish. It was comical, terrifying.

And that's how it went—endless Sagueiros, infinite Assicantes, always enough chairs. Always eighteen, new Madlock avatars replacing the fallen.

Sam's team pressed on amidst it all, made the ATVs by mid-afternoon, reached Baylieu at 0720 the next morning, leaving their strange bodyguards to stop, stand watching, then vanish within view of the famous Gate.

And the first thing Sam did after the debrief was file an official request to have The Madlock be renamed The Go-Between. The second was to send out a call to his flash crew to assemble for a full active-phase mission.

In the midst of changing worlds, the world had changed in a way that gave just enough hope—for a future, some kind of viable future for the race. Dangerous, always dangerous, going out among the Landings, but he meant to give others a taste of what *this* was. Patches on wounds.

The Australian Landings

1.	The Quintain	18.	The Caress
2.	The Never-Fail	19.	Dancing Doris
3.	The Four-Mile	20.	The Lucky Boatmen
4.	The Flower Seller	21.	The Horse
5.	The Queen's House	22.	The Sailmaker
6.	The Old Angel	23.	The Sailmaker II (Redux)
7.	The Early Riser	24.	The Spanish Lantern
8.	The Night Tree	25.	The Moonraker
9.	The Sidewinder	26.	The Three Spices
10.	The Blue Ship	27.	The Quilter
11.	The Lover	28.	The Four Doormen
12.	The Dormeuse	29.	The Firewalker
13.	The Station Master	30.	The Madlock
14.	The Provocator	31.	The Praying Hands
15.	The Aviator	32.	The Breakwater
16.	The Pure	33.	The Pearl
17.	The Arete		

The Author: Terry Dowling
Terry Dowling is one of Australia's most respected and internationally acclaimed writers of science fiction, dark fantasy and horror, and author of the multi-award-winning Tom Rynosseros saga. He has been called 'Australia's finest writer of horror' by *Locus* magazine, its 'premier writer of dark fantasy' by *All Hallows* and its 'most acclaimed writer of the dark fantastic' by *Cemetery Dance* magazine. Terry's new collection *The Night Shop: Tales for the Lonely Hours* is due from Cemetery Dance Publications in 2017. His homepage is at www.terrydowling.com.

Story Behind the Story
'The Madlock Chair' is set in the same future Australia as my 2003 story 'Flashmen' (which Gardner Dozois took for The Year's Best Science Fiction in 2004). That story never needed any kind of follow-up, but the Landings are such a fascinating global phenomenon and Sam 'Aitch' Aitchander such an interesting character that I kept being drawn back to them. One of the greatest challenges SF presents, as I see it, is to create a sense of the truly alien, then show how humanity ranges itself against it as a way of measuring that humanity. Compiling this list of the Australian Landings did the rest. How could I keep away?

The Illustrator: Kate Harrison
Kate Harrison is a Melbourne-based artist; born in 1982 she spent much of her childhood drawing and reading science fiction/fantasy obsessively. No longer studying illustration, Kate has graduated from starving student to starving artist and spends most of her free time devoted to reading, boxing and cat maintenance.

Illustration by Sarah Carapace

All We Have Is Us

Alex Isle

Ella never had a real job before the end of the world. Now she scavenged through the city's once-rich houses to pay her way. This house had been gone over before, but people of her youth and small size often had to settle for remains.

She got in easily via the front door, its lock already broken and found dust and broken pieces of stone and glass lying around what had been a white marble floor. *There's always stuff the big folk don't want*, Ella reminded herself, and set herself to exploring all three levels of the huge house. She found two skeletons on the second floor, almost hidden in the filthy remains of a thick golden carpet. There was a scattering of electronic bits around them, like somebody had smashed a tablet computer or smartphone on the wall, maybe.

Ella even checked the kitchen, though food that was edible was even less likely than tradeable junk. She found nothing, and sat down despondently on a clean spot near the kitchen door.

What else? Had she missed anything at all or skimped where she should have looked more closely? Ella sighed and let herself slide down to the tiled floor—only the kitchen had no carpet—and stretched out to let herself rest for a moment, a small, skinny shape in the dim light. She lay on her back, her head against the floor, staring up at nothing, her pack beside her within easy grabbing distance. There was a thudding against the back of her skull, faint and distant, the slightest shuddering of the floor. Ella sat up in sudden panic, for such noises could mean a big herd of shamblers and even if they didn't know she was there yet, that could mean real problems getting back to base.

She made her way to the front of the house and looked out from the half open door. Scent trail—she would have left that, even someone her size could ring the dinner bell for shamblers. She couldn't see any, or any person who might have led some shamblers here, and after a few careful minutes waiting, went back inside and lay down on the tiles with her ear to the floor. Again she could hear—feel—the thudding sounds of feet, or blows.

Likeliest, she thought, was that someone had trapped a shambler, maybe back when they were still saying it was only a disease and you could get better. Even after they'd stopped saying you should take them to the hospital. Some people kept their infected family members, but they had to make sure they couldn't attack them. So maybe there *was* a room below that no-one had ever found. One shambler, she could deal with.

She stood and moved to the wall, tapping almost idly along it and listening to the sounds she made. She was almost the entire length of the outer side of the passage when the sounds changed to hollowness. Ella knocked a fist against the whitewashing to be sure and stumbled back in shock when her fist broke through the apparent solidity of the wall.

In the games she had once loved to play, when there had been computers with bright graphics and clanging music, there was always a hidden tunnel. She listened carefully before she began to break the pieces of wall, enough for her to sidle into the dark passage.

* * *

There was light. Ella had not expected that, though she hadn't thought about how she'd see in the windowless tunnel, with no torch or lighter, but when she had moved only a few paces, she could see another break, this one an actual doorway left open a few centimetres, and from it flooded artificial light. She was in a small cramped passage, with a heavy metal door in front of her, and Ella groaned; there was no way she could force her way past that. She'd have to go and get some of the others and then share whatever was inside with them, if they even threw her any scraps after she did that. But she gripped her knife tightly, reminding herself that there could still be a shambler and it might not be on the other side of that door.

She reached out to touch the door and hesitated. There was a sort of pad on it, metal and plastic, with five indentations as if one were meant to splay one's hand out against it. It shouldn't work anymore. It would need electrics. But the light worked and it shouldn't. She jumped as her palm touched cool metal, but no current of death shot through her. Instead, the big door slid sideways with a rattle and she was looking into more passageway, this one intact, dusty but clean, with another door two paces away.

Still there was silence and it drew Ella's curiosity, step by step below the unnerving lights. She put her head against the door to listen to the room beyond—still nothing—before turning the doorknob as quietly as she could. It opened easily. In this room too there was light, inexplicable and alien, and below it, facing her, stood a human form.

* * *

The eyes looking back at her didn't belong to a shambler.

The woman was maybe eight or ten years older than her. Ella couldn't tell for sure; her skin was so weirdly pale and unmarked. She was wearing a loose sort of dress that fell in folds of silky blue cloth to her feet. Emerging from it, her wrists were bony and her face hollow. Dark hair was tied back in a long, lank tail at her neck.

They stared at one another. Ella's gaze flicked from the woman's face to examine the room behind her. It was cluttered with apparent junk—a scavenger's potential paradise, but it appeared to be the woman's home. Ella spotted a bed, loaded with clothing and covers, cupboards, dusty blankets flung in a heap, books balanced on top of one another reaching as high as the ceiling. *Books*. Ella stared at them for a long time, then reluctantly back to the woman, who hadn't moved. Not salvage, not with the owner here, and one on one, she was too small to risk a fight.

'Did he send you?'

The woman's voice was a husk, the lowest of whispers, and she quickly looked away from Ella's face.

'No-one sent me,' Ella said, reassured by the words that she really wasn't dealing with some weird variety of shambler. 'I didn't know anyone was in the house; it's abandoned. Lot of scavengers been through before me and they didn't know anyone was here. You, uh, live here with somebody?'

'The man,' she said, with a slight nod. She frowned suddenly and Ella caught a glimpse of a *person* there. 'I… I'm supposed to introduce myself. My name is Iveta. It's very nice to meet you.' She stuck out her bony hand and Ella gingerly touched it, the brown of her own skin making Iveta's hand look like a ghostly claw. Iveta jumped. Despite the rote words, she wasn't at all used to meeting someone.

'Uh, hi. My name's Ella.'

'How old are you?'

There was no shortage of folk running around without their fair quota of brains, whether they had started off that way or whether, when the deadflu came along, they couldn't handle it. Ella was well on the way to classifying Iveta with them. 'The man' must have been her jailer and it looked like he had been gone awhile. One thing Ella couldn't spot was any food, though there was a stack of dirty utensils in a corner sink.

'I'm fourteen,' she responded, as she would to a younger kid. 'How old are you?'

Iveta frowned. 'I was twelve when he took me and I don't remember how long ago that was. He's never let me know days or years. Did you bring me my meal?'

'When did he take you?'

'Oh eight.'

'2008?'

'Yes.'

'That's… ten years before the deadflu year.'

Iveta didn't react, it was as though the words were meaningless to her, but after a moment she said curiously, 'So it's 2018 now?'

Ella shook her head. '2020. Two years ago everything fell apart. So, there weren't any shamblers when you came here?' Ella's voice rose in excitement and Iveta moved back quickly as though she feared the younger girl. 'Is this right? Somebody put you here?'

'He took me,' Iveta answered. 'I was on my way to school and I was nervous because I had a maths test. So I was going over my times tables to myself and not watching where I was going. He was driving a van and just pulled up beside me, jumped out and grabbed me. It hurt when he threw me into the van and I screamed till I couldn't talk, but he… I remember going into this big, gorgeous house and down some stairs and in here. Is it all right to talk to you about that? He's not going to be mad that I talked to you? Only he's been gone for so long.'

'There's nobody in the house,' was all Ella could think of to say. 'Look, you need to come out with me. I'll find you something to eat. Do you want to bring anything?'

'No.'

Iveta didn't even look at the mass of things cramped into the room. Ella took a careful breath. It technically meant this wealth of pre-flu stuff was abandoned and she could claim. But if they left the house and someone else came in through the way she'd broken open, that wasn't going to mean a thing.

Iveta followed her, doing exactly what Ella said, so much so that it began to creep Ella out. She stopped many times and needed some persuasion to keep going. In the tunnel was all right but when they finally emerged into the kitchen, Iveta panicked and started screeching so loudly that Ella could *feel* those shamblers' pricking up what passed for their ears and turning this way. 'Iveta, please stop, you're going to—STOP!'

She hadn't meant to be quite that loud herself, but Iveta did stop, suddenly, drawing into herself with a frightened whimper and pressing against the side of the tunnel, looking out into a room twice the size of her lair and totally unfamiliar. When Ella tried to awkwardly pat her arm, she shrieked again and then lunged at her, grabbing her so tight around the neck she could hardly breathe. Still, it seemed to do the trick. Moments later Iveta eased her hold and Ella gasped until she got her breath back, still closely held in Iveta's stick thin arms.

'We got to keep quiet,' Ella managed to say. 'There's shamblers—they look like people, kind of, but people that are falling apart, and they want to eat you. They happened around two years ago when the flu came and, well, things got a lot different. I was on the street already, so I could manage pretty well and I can manage for you if you keep doing what I say. Okay?'

'Okay. Can I have something to eat?'

'I'm going to find us something, but I need you to wait here. You can sit here in the wall. Here.' Ella pulled her water bottle from her pack and handed it over. 'It's just water but it's clean. I'll be back with some food, soon as.'

Iveta nodded obediently, but asked, 'What if the man comes? I'm not supposed to be out.'

If the man is alive, he's a survivor like the rest of us. He would know the rules. But he's not alive now or he'd still feed her, wouldn't he? Ella looked at the pale, unlined face, the eyes which appeared blank at first, but there had been that flash of the original Iveta—what she'd been before somebody had made her into a thing inside the walls. If she woke up again, she could make it. 'He's not going to come.' Ella spoke as authoritatively as she could, channelling any one of the top-level survivors who managed the trading and rewards for what street rats like her brought in. If she was ever going to be one of them, it was time she learned the manner. 'But if *anyone* but me comes, this is what to say, okay?' A nod. 'You tell them Ella and Iveta are holding this place and it's taken. Just that. Can you say that back?'

Iveta said it. Ella drew her small knife, wincing. She always hated this bit. She sliced her finger sharply, drawing a gasp from Iveta, and stepped closer to the wall to smear the flowing blood in a rough pattern of a circle with a line through it.

'Okay. You point to that after you say the words. Now you wait.'

It might not work; it didn't always. People were people and there were gangs out there that took stuff to use themselves and raided or even killed living people. But enough followed the salvage rules, and those said that even if it was a skinny fourteen-year-old kid and a woman who looked like a pale, bony ghost, they kept what they took. 'All we have is us.' That was scrawled on the wall in the building—the lair—where Kendra and the rest of the mob Ella was loosely aligned with lived.

When Ella got outside, she was dismayed to see how low the sun was. She'd taken longer than she thought and night couldn't be far away. The shamblers were more active at night, maybe because it was summer and the heat slowed them down same as it did the living people, or maybe it just seemed that way because you couldn't see them till they got close. With fresh ones it could be hard to make out whether they were living folks or not, and no matter how careful you tried to be, there were always fresh ones.

The lair was hours walk away across the burbs in what had been trendy West Perth, even if she got them fuelled first. The hollow, fuzzy feeling. She had told her she'd need to eat before she did much more, and it looked like Iveta was already past that point. Might be she'd move easier at night, though. But not till she gets food in, Ella thought. She had already checked most of the places around here on her own account and she didn't have the strength for a long hunt. It was going to have to be rats. Or mice.

She was scratched and bleeding by the time she got back. Crawling in the dusty, splintery roof space of a house after agile rodents tended to do that to a person. Still, her blood lured them and she would have had to cut herself if the wooden beams she crawled over hadn't done the job for her. She had pockets full of squashed mice by the time she climbed down.

Iveta didn't make a fuss about being asked to eat raw mice. Not at all. She simply took what Ella handed her, popped them in and chewed. Her expression didn't alter from a vague stare as she did. Ella was learning that that was the woman's default. When Ella spoke to her, Iveta focused with alarming intensity and that was when you saw flashes of the 'real Iveta' but otherwise, she lapsed into this nowhere state.

'Did you see any live people?' Ella asked when the grisly meal was done. 'No.'

'Any deadfolk? Shamblers?'

'No.'

Nor had Ella, coming back, but she had heard the moans being carried on the night breeze. Some of the others, the older people, had detailed theories about just why the shamblers happened, and as many theories as there were survivors. Most folk believed the last flu epidemic had been involved somehow. Enough believed, that it became known as deadflu, though it mostly didn't kill you by itself. But if you'd had it, when you died, whenever you died, you got up as a shambler. It only took one elderly person to die of natural causes and start biting.

After that, not a lot happened in an orderly manner.

Ella, as a teenaged street kid, hadn't cared about the science at the time, just about avoiding the people stricken by this weird new drug that sent them crazy and hungry. She didn't care now. They could stay till morning, she thought, except she didn't trust Iveta to keep a reliable lookout and it was still possible that shamblers were close by. They could go dormant if there was nothing to eat, but if a meal happened by, they woke up fast.

'We need to get back to my friends,' she told Iveta. 'We have to walk and it's dark. Can you do that?'

'He took me,' Iveta whispered. 'I was walking to school and he grabbed me and my family don't know where I am. Can I please call them?'

'There's no phones,' Ella said. 'I don't have any. We can try to find them. My friends will help. But we have to walk a long way in the dark. Can you do that?'

'But you're not much older than me,' Iveta said, confused. 'Kids don't wander in the dark on their own, it's too dangerous.' Again that flash, the remembered fear in her eyes. 'Can't we call a taxi? My parents will pay the driver when we get to my house.'

She wasn't remembering the ten years, Ella thought. She thought she was still twelve or whatever it was. 'There aren't any taxis. We've got to walk but I know the way. It'll be all right. You just have to do what I say.'

Iveta didn't stop talking, or whispering, as she followed Ella so closely she almost tripped her up a few times. Ella gave up hushing her, it didn't work and only added to the sounds. 'Mt Claremont,' Iveta hissed. 'That's where we are. There's a bus stop down here. Can't we catch a bus if you can't call a taxi? Straight into the city.'

'Only if you want to die,' Ella said at last, pulling her into the shelter of the large bushes that grew along the roadside.

She sniffed—only the pungent smell of oleander, no deadfolk. 'There are no buses or taxis or trains, Iveta. We have to walk, remember?' And so it went on, the prickling of nerves along Ella's neck never easing. She took the path that led her to the old railway, where a derailed train still lay shattered beside the tracks. There was a secured carriage where they could hide out. There might be somebody already there but that should be all right. It was a truce zone, and about the same number of people respected that as did the rule of salvage.

Then she heard the moans, the sounds which were no more than air pushed through lungs, no mind behind them. She grabbed Iveta's arm to hold her still and put her hand briefly over her mouth saying, 'Quiet!'

They waited as the deadfolk shambled across their path. Iveta gasped slightly as the stench reached her. Ella had known to breathe through her mouth—no-one ever got used to that stink—but she hadn't thought to warn the woman. She had never expected to meet anyone who was not a survivor. Who didn't know *anything* of the world.

There wasn't much light; the moon was overcast and clouds drifted, obscuring the stars. It had made it easier to move Iveta, making the woman feel as though she was still in a large room, with visibility only a few metres. But there was enough to discern that the creatures shuffling ahead of them were no longer right, no longer human. They were old ones too, their remaining skin reduced to leather hanging from bones. The stench came from their feeding rather than the shamblers themselves. Three, four, five of them, and Ella's grip remained on Iveta. Finally, the creatures were gone and Ella let out her breath.

'*Zombies?* Those were really zombies—like the movies? But why don't you shoot them?'

'What with?' the younger girl asked. 'Even if we had a gun, the noise would just bring packs of them on us. The guns never worked, Iveta.'

Iveta took a step forward and Ella halted her again. 'Wait. If we keep going, they'll pick up our scent. There's a breeze now, can't you feel it? We have to wait.'

* * *

Iveta was nearly dropping with fatigue before they reached the railway and the dark mass of the wrecked train. Ella felt weary herself; she'd expected to be home and able to sleep long before this, not having to lead someone more awkward and larger than she was through the wreckage to the safe hole. The train carriage didn't look secure and she had to push in behind a heavy sheet of metal to find the entrance. Once in, there was nothing but the metal hole itself, a lair to crouch in and try to rest, to come down from shivering alert enough to sleep, while the night blew and moaned outside.

In the pearly gray light of dawn, they moved again, two figures picking their way through the debris of city suburbia. Iveta held tight to Ella's hand and even shut her eyes for some of it. Her fear had silenced her. Ella herself was starting to worry, now that she saw the helplessness of the woman. Would the salvage be enough for the others to accept her? All of them had survived because they had something more than most people, never mind age or race or origin: a pig-headed determination not to let anyone else tell them what the hell they could do. It looked like whoever had held Iveta might be one of them, unless he was one of those skeletons trapped in the thick carpet of that home.

It was going to hit Ella's own status, if she defended Iveta. She was still worrying at this, when she all but dragged Iveta through the door of her home and worked her hand free of the woman's painfully tight grip. She ignored Iveta's childlike cry of alarm. 'Stand there!'

* * *

The sentry had seen that she was pulling Iveta rather than being under duress herself. That was the only reason the woman hadn't been speared or stabbed already, and Ella knew better than to bring her any further inside than the entrance to their building. It had been offices once, not a home, but there were no offices now and the place was sturdy, made more secure by their alterations. Metal barricades now stood where open sheets of glass had once displayed the interior to the world. No-one lived on the ground floor. It was the final layer of protection.

Iveta cried out in panic as people appeared from the stairwell and followed them in from outside. She threw herself at Ella and hugged the girl painfully tight, despite Ella's efforts to extricate herself or make Iveta let go. 'It's okay, she's not hurting me,' Ella called. 'She's scared!'

'Back off, people,' a recognised voice called back. 'Honestly, it's like seagulls when you scatter food on the ground!'

Several minutes later, after talking quietly and firmly to Iveta, Ella got her to ease her grip and stood there, rubbing her neck with a grimace. Iveta started as a big, dark-skinned woman came forward to them, holding her empty hands out reassuringly. 'It's all right. We're friends. My name is Kendra and I'm a friend of your friend there.'

Iveta blinked in alarm as the second new human in years came to a stop within arm's reach from her. Unlike Ella, Kendra was taller than she was and sturdily built, wearing a loose tunic and trousers. Inside clothing. Outside, no-one wore anything that shamblers could grab. For that same reason, her black shaggy hair was cropped as short as Ella's.

Kendra studied her in return with obvious unease and flicked a look at Ella. *We need to talk.* 'What's your name?' the woman asked Iveta.

'My name is Iveta. It's very nice to meet you,' Iveta blurted out, though her eyes were still wide with fear.

'Is it?' Kendra asked, mildly amused. 'I'm sure you need to rest. I'm going to ask Ella to take you to her spot and then she and I need to have a chat.'

Iveta accepted this as writ, just as she had anything Ella told her. She let Ella grasp her arm and lead her towards the stairwell, climbing with reasonable alacrity and only skittering a few times when they passed other dwellers standing on the stairs to watch her.

'Is Kendra your boss?' Iveta followed Ella onto a second floor landing. They passed doors where people stood, looking and whispering about the weird looking newcomer. Not much changed day to day and someone this strange was a new and interesting thing.

'She runs this group,' Ella said. 'I'm not one of hers, exactly. I like to do my own thing, but I have to mind her rules.' That clearly made sense to Iveta, who nodded quickly. 'She could kick me out if I make trouble. So we have to be quiet here and do jobs when they tell us.' She turned towards a closed door and fumbled it open; her fatigue was getting bad. Beyond was a small storage-type room with roller shelves still in place. Now they held Ella's gear. On the floor was her mattress and bedding, to which she guided Iveta.

'You can stay here. Here's a water bottle and some food.' She retrieved a bag of dried fruit scraps from a shelf and handed it over, a bit reluctantly. If things went south as regards to the salvage, she would have to move quickly to get more rations. She grabbed a handful of the dried fruit to munch as she headed back downstairs, where Kendra would certainly be waiting for her.

'Where in all creation did you find her?' was the leader's immediate question, as she examined Ella thoughtfully. They were in Kendra's library, essentially her living quarters, but crammed with so many books that it was more their room than hers.

'She was in a hidden room,' Ella said and briefly described how she had discovered it and gotten in. 'Someone put her there when she was younger than me. She hasn't said how long he's been gone but long enough for her to get hungry. He could be in a group somewhere.'

'We can't very well interrogate everyone to find out if they had a secret... pet that they abandoned,' Kendra commented. 'So, can she do anything?'

'Well, she got here with me even though, if she's telling the truth, she hasn't travelled anywhere outside for half her life,' Ella said uncomfortably, then trailed off as screams reached her ears. She and Kendra immediately raced for the door, following the sounds upstairs, where they grew painfully intense, right to the door of Ella's room, which was open and clustered with three of her neighbours.

'Out of the way, you morons!' Ella yelled, elbowing one, which earned her a cuff across the head from Kendra, who delivered the same impartially to another of the onlookers. With the way cleared, they got through the doorway and saw the shrieking Iveta, curled into fetal position against the far wall.

'Go on,' Kendra said. Ella didn't at all want to attract the woman's attention but she had no choice. It took crouching down and shaking Iveta to eventually get her far out of her zone of blind panic to notice that Ella was there, whereupon she latched on with the same child-to-parent intensity as before. Her shrieks died down to gasps for breath and sobs and her fingers cut painfully into Ella's thin shoulders.

'What happened?' Ella asked several times before Iveta was calm enough to respond. She had babbled about 'where's the room, he's going to come, where is he?' without seeming to recognise Ella, but now looked at her.

'They opened it, they came in, they came in and *looked*,' she blurted.

'She was already yelling her head off for you,' one of the onlookers said in indignant justification. 'I was just gonna talk to her and calm her down. She's going to bring all the shamblers in Perth on us with that stupid noise.'

'You're stupid,' Ella retorted.

'All right, that's enough. You three go about your own business if you actually have any,' Kendra ordered. When they were gone and the room quiet, she sat down cross-legged on the floor and waved at Ella. 'You sit, get her to do the same. That's it. Look, Ivy…'

'Iveta.'

'Iveta. I know you're confused and in the world before, we'd call the police and they would find your family and get a counsellor for you. We can't do that,' Kendra added quickly before Iveta latched on to the mention of her family. 'The city's in ruins. The government disappeared over a year ago and we don't have a clue what's going on outside Perth. They could be ignoring us. We could be the last outpost. Don't know. But like the sign says, we're all you've got, so you need to calm down and pay attention. You're like a time traveller; you went forward ten years or whatever it is and when you came out, everything was different. You ever read stories like that?'

'He brought me books,' Iveta said.

Ella saw Kendra's head lift with interest at the mention of books and secretly rejoiced. Once Ella got the credit for bringing in that library here, she would be coasting for months.

'He—whatever his name is—is gone,' Kendra said bluntly. 'Probably dead. Ella said there were bones in the house where she found you, the bones of two people. Didn't this guy tell you anything about what was happening outside?'

'He wanted me to be pure,' Iveta whispered.

'Do you know his name?'

Iveta did not. He was simply 'he' or 'the man', which she said with trembling fear and a glance around as though her jailer might appear at any moment. Nor could Kendra and Ella elicit anything in the way of a personal description or behaviour that could identify what sounded like a pretty serious loony, as Kendra muttered under her breath to Ella. Not anyone they wanted around their survivor group. Though he could have been around for the past decade, happily living his two lives.

'All right,' Kendra said at last to Ella. 'I wanted to talk to you on your own but I guess that won't work, not for the moment. You were going to tell me what use your friend might be.'

'There's a stash,' Ella said, cutting to it direct, bringing the important stuff up quickly before something or somebody else got Kendra's attention. 'Books and house stuff and blankets all crammed in the room where I found her. House has been cleared, but no-one ever found the room, it looks like. No food, so this guy hasn't been bringing her meals for a while. There were plates with dried mess on them and empty tins, is all I know. We claim salvage,' she said in a rush. 'Iveta and me.'

'If you claim her, that cuts your share. You do know that?'

'Not *her*. She's not mine, my...'

'Not your dependent, you mean? She's not your equal partner, Ella, that's crazy. We can't claim that when anyone who sees her will know she's...' Kendra's hand made a circling motion near her ear. Iveta didn't seem to know she was being discussed, nor did she seem to care. She sat next to Ella, clutching her hand. 'No. You've found good salvage, that's great. But if you also bring a survivor who can't do anything to help us, that's a step back and she's not entitled to a full share. Half yours or nothing, it's up to you.'

'You'll help bring the stuff from the room here?'

'Yes. But it cuts into your share,' Kendra repeated, patient and adamant. 'And keep trying to get a description of the guy. I'd really like to know if we have a slave-keeping psycho among us. Just saying.'

* * *

Iveta panicked when she saw a man. Any man. Which didn't help to narrow down the search at all. She wouldn't move from Ella's side, even camping outside the lavatories or the showers. Ella had a few fights with people who decided this was funny and made comments, until Kendra threatened to throw them outside and let them play with the deadfolk.

Ella thought about just taking her share and moving on, when they got the junk from Iveta's cell back here and traded or distributed. She'd hung around on the edge of Kendra's community since things fell apart, which some defined as the time the government disappeared. Others timed it from when the internet, no longer managed or maintained, finally went down and didn't rise—unlike three quarters of the Western Australian citizenry, but Ella, in the foster system from her earliest memories and a street kid since twelve or so, had never shared that fixation beyond a love of computer games.

Iveta had never been allowed internet in her long years underneath that house, and had only foggy memories of playing games with a screen before she was taken. She'd studied a lot, she said, and the man had encouraged this. Kendra, relieved to find something useful in the frail young woman's head, got her to try teaching the younger children, with Ella as reluctant supervisor. Letters and times tables, Kendra said. Everyone needs that. And she drummed her knuckles on Ella's head when Ella muttered about not *everyone.* The entire group, not just Kendra and Ella, were startled when their newest arrival turned out to be good at this, enough that the kids began to be actually interested in learning.

They had to wait two days for a shambler herd to disperse before they could travel to Iveta's prison. 'You can wait here for us,' Ella told her taller shadow, but this thought seemed to terrify Iveta.

'I need to go with you,' she insisted to Ella, in front of the group of heartlessly amused survivors in the bare lobby of their building. 'What if the man comes here?'

'The people here will make sure he doesn't.'

'Give it up, Ella,' Kendra growled. 'We're going to be here for hours and still not get anywhere. Make sure she keeps up and doesn't squawk. And try to trust me, all right?'

Kendra had never before personally led a salvage team for anything Ella had found, but she told the younger girl she couldn't get the idea of the hidden cell out of her mind and wanted to see it for herself. The location might also give a clue as to the man's identity. Kendra knew quite a bit about her fellow survivors, anything they were prepared to give up. 'I was a librarian,' she said, not for the first time. 'I know how to organise and I know how to talk to people.'

They moved silently through the outside world. Not chatting had been one of the harder things for the survivors to learn. The deadfolk homed in on any noise, particularly noise from the delicious living things they had once been. Ella and Kendra had had to run for their lives several times while some shambler closed in on someone who couldn't keep their mouth shut. There was a lot less of that these days.

The area had once been a trendy part of the city: offices blending with expensive apartments, boutiques and coffee shops along the line of the railway. Constant culling kept the roadways mostly clear, though new ones kept wandering in, or old ones circled. Ella had never paid much attention to the old buildings—they'd been gutted early on—and even now she looked only to make sure there were no lurkers. For Iveta, though, the destruction and devastation was as fresh as a bleeding bite mark.

When she drew breath to cry out for the dozenth time, Ella closed on her and smacked her hand across Iveta's mouth. 'If you had yelled,' she murmured, not whispering, since that carried further, 'Kendra or someone would have probably hit you. You *got* to be quiet.'

Ella didn't miss the glances the five others in the group exchanged with one another. They were of the *this loot had better be good* variety.

The sun was hot on Ella's face and everywhere else. It sucked the moisture out of everything around them, including the seven humans themselves, slinking like feral cats through the remains of their city. Even though Ella had made sure Iveta ate and drank well before they left, the young woman was struggling to keep up. Her pale skin was reddened where the sun struck it and by the way she was walking in the old sneakers Ella had found for her, she had blisters. Ella went barefoot a lot of the time, like now, but Iveta's feet were soft and pale and would have been torn to shreds. Ella had trouble imagining all the deadfolk as being like Iveta, but they really had been, not so long ago.

She thought about the skeletons she'd seen at the house, the way they looked like they'd grown into the carpet and the fallen-in state of the bones. Over the last two years, she'd become as expert as anyone at deciphering them. They were approaching the house when she said quietly to Kendra, 'They're too old.'

'What are?'

'The skeletons. Iveta would be dead if one of them was him, because no-one would have been feeding her.'

Kendra began to answer and then five people emerged from the house and spread out slightly to wait for them. In their group, Ella stopped and jerked on Iveta's arm to make her halt as well, so that only Kendra stepped out ahead of them to meet the leader of the others. There could be more people inside of the house. It would be dumb to assume that they outnumbered these folk.

'We've got this place,' the male leader said to Kendra. He was big, maybe in his forties, with a brindled beard of grey and brown, and knew how to use his size to intimidate, standing close enough to look down at her. There was a knife and machete at his belt but he hadn't reached for them.

'My girl here claimed salvage two days ago. Her sign's on the wall inside. She claims what's in the room beyond it. You get the rest of the house.'

The man looked at Ella in a way that made her want to shrink away. Then he turned his shoulder to Kendra and beckoned his people closer. They talked in a quick whisper and then one of them disappeared back into the house.

'We've been guided here by the owner,' the leader said. 'That was before the sign was placed, so you can't claim.' His follower came back out and another person after her, at the sight of whom Iveta gasped and went stiff with fear. Ella felt her hand gripped so tightly it seemed her bones would break.

This man was nothing unusual: smaller than the leader and paler, not ghostlike the way Iveta was, but certainly he'd been able to avoid the sun. He was plumper than the usual survivor, his hair scant over his scalp, and his eyes were shielded with spectacles. He wore the ruins of a white dress shirt and loose, holey trousers. And he stared at Iveta so intently that neither Ella nor Kendra had to wonder who he was. Or what.

'She's mine,' he whispered. 'I can prove it. I can tell you exactly what's inside there. I can show you things she wrote and drew and put her name on them. Ask her the name. It'll prove what I say.'

Ella hoped that Iveta would argue or at least refuse to say, but she didn't. 'Iveta Castain,' she said, staring back at the man. One of the other survivor group went back inside and soon came out, bearing a ragged piece of paper with a childish drawing on it: a man seated at a table, eating something with knife and fork. Iveta's name was scrawled beneath the sketch.

'Have you been in there like a damn spider, just eating your supplies up?' Kendra demanded. 'Get low on food, did you, so you went out looking for helpers?' The other leader and his two people clearly didn't like this description. The bearded man scowled at Kendra, while Ella looked from one face to another, not sure what was going on. She started to speak, to say Iveta was *her* salvage—surely better that than letting the man get her back—but Kendra made a cutting motion at her. *Shut up.*

Another of Kendra's people, a tall woman named Jess, was moving behind the man. Her motion vague as though she just happened to be drifting that way.

'He's not one of yours, is he?' Kendra said to the other leader, who shook his head slightly. 'Yeah. We know he's not. He left this girl locked in there to die, while he went looking for another meal ticket. Gods know how you found him before the shamblers did.'

'He was yelling out for the police,' the leader admitted, causing a low ripple of laughter from his group and Kendra's. 'We thought he was crazy, so we took him away and had to wait three days for him to calm down. But he never said anyone else was here.'

'She's *mine*,' the man said, whined really. He reached to grab Iveta's arm and she just stood there. It was Ella who tried to make him let go, until the other leader glared at her.

'He took a child,' Kendra said, pointing at Iveta to show who she meant by the child. 'Ten years before the deadflu and everything else. Kept her in an underground room where my girl found her and brought her out. This young woman may not know anything about living here now, but she knows things from before and she's been teaching our children. She could help your children too, if they need a teacher.'

'You'd let our children learn from her?' another of the rival group asked in surprise.

'Sure. We keep her, we take the books, you take anything else. We organise classes for our kids and yours.'

'Hey!' the man complained. 'I'm the one who knows useful stuff from before. And it's my house here, my belongings that I've hidden all this time, that I'm giving to *you* in return for you looking out for me…'

Ella barely saw the nod from Kendra. No-one could miss the glint of the machete in Jess's hand, raised swiftly and lowered in a swooping cut against the man's neck. He crumpled silently to the ground, and continued to bleed, for several minutes. No-one moved from either group, until Kendra said, 'Make sure,' to Jess, and Jess did.

Someone sighed audibly and then everyone relaxed. The two leaders shrugged at one another and Kendra shot a brief smile at Ella. 'You need to trust your elders a bit more,' she said, and to the bearded man, 'You followed him in good faith. You couldn't know he wasn't right. So we'll split the salvage as I said, if that suits you.'

She nodded at the still body, but the other leader grimaced. 'Don't know any who would want *that*,' he said. 'Let's get the salvage out here and then we can sort out this schooling for our kids.'

'Education's what will bring us together,' Kendra agreed.

'Until somebody comes to help us,' he murmured.

'Until then,' Kendra said.

She made a 'stay here' sign to Ella and both the leaders went into the house. Ella sighed. She had just seen her independence disappear. Maybe no-one else had seen it, but Kendra had just claimed her as part of her group's rights. Iveta, the time traveller, might be the most valuable thing achieved that day, but Iveta was going to need Ella in order for the whole agreement to work.

It could be such a pain to live in a civilised world.

The Author: Alex Isle

Alex Isle lives in Perth and plans its (fictional) destruction on a regular basis. Alex has been published in various publications including *Sword and Sorceress*, *Andromeda Spaceways Magazine*, *Southern Blood*, Twelfth Planet Press publications (primarily the short story collection *Nightsiders*), *Orb*, *Agog*, and of course *Aurealis*, in various issues including number 1! Alex also wrote a fantasy novel, *Scale of Dragon, Tooth of Wolf* and *Wolf Children*, a dramatised non-fiction account of children raised by wolves.

Story Behind the Story

I realised that I'd never written a story with zombies, although I enjoy the genre. Or a story about a nutcase who keeps a prisoner for many years in a hidden room, though such things are unfortunately not fictional. What value would such a prisoner have to the few who managed to survive the disintegration of their society, and what values would they maintain in a world where they're a prey species? 'All We Have Is Us' was the result of such introspection.

It tells the story of a teenager, because they're on the edge of adult society anyway, and because I think that a teenager could best understand the mind of someone shut away as a child, so never able to become a true adult, someone out of time because the collapse of society that happened in her absence.

The Illustrator: Sarah Carapace

Sarah Carapace is a Melbourne-based artist who draws punk girls, bug monsters and cyborg crabs. She likes milkshakes, body horror and will never be over Cyberpunk ever. You can find more of her art at sarahcarapace.tumblr.com.

DO

Forest/Trees

Illustration by Lynette Watters

Forest/Trees

Stephen Higgins

'Do not think for a minute that I am happy about this,' Tier said. 'I'm supposed to be on a flight for a meeting.'

Alan checked the comp again. There was definitely no power connected to it. He had a thorough rummage around the back of the comp and ensured that there were no leads at all. There wasn't. There weren't even any unplugged leads.

'Nothing,' he said.

'There must be something?' Tier replied. 'It's still on the screen. Check for wireless or powerpods or something.'

Alan sighed. He stood and looked around the room. Tier was by the window, absently looking out as he texted someone. The room was shabby. It had the detritus of misuse scattered about: scraps of paper, an empty cardboard box, an old office chair with one castor missing, and there was the computer and monitor sitting on old table. The monitor had a faint glow emanating from it. In the centre of the screen was the word 'Do'. There was also a dead bird in one corner of the room. And there was Alan, and Alan had the feeling that this was pretty much the order of priorities as far as Tier was concerned.

As Alan ran a scanner over the walls of the room, Tier was busy issuing instructions to people. The instructions had that perfunctory tone that people used when they were accustomed to having their orders followed. Tier wanted news of another meeting that was taking place somewhere else. He wanted news about an investment he hoped to make. He wanted to change the time of an appointment, and he wanted to know why Alan had dragged him up here. It took a moment for Alan to realise that Tier had put his mobile away and was looking at him expectantly.

'Well?' Tier asked. 'It's just a computer screen. Obviously there must be some source of power to it and it's been left on. I can't see the problem, and I can't see the reason why you asked me to come here.'

Alan wasn't really sure himself. It had just seemed odd. He had come to decommission the nanotech that had been sifted into the plantation. The plantation had started off as an energy source. The trees had been 'etched' to provide electricity via the leaves that had been teched into so many solar panels. It was old tech but still useful. Well, still useful until Tier had realised that there was more money to be had from subdividing the land and selling the plots. Alan and Linda Frents had been the only two employees and Linda had left when she saw the way Tier was thinking. Alan had remained to shut down the plantation and sell off as much of the tech as possible. He had binned most of the comp hardware, but there was still this one technological dinosaur left. And now it had a flickering screen with a Word doc open and the word 'Do' in a large font. And no apparent power supply.

Alan wondered if now was a good time to mention the ghosts. He thought not.

'There's no power supply to that computer or that monitor,' he said. 'I've checked and rechecked and there simply isn't. I called you because I thought you might like to see what's going on here before we just left it to be divided up. There's something wrong here.'

Tier sighed. He liked Alan. He really did but he could be a pain. He always got into a state about minor problems.

'So can't there be a sort of remnant of power left in the screen or something like that? I know what you're going to say but bear with me… All that nanotech up here forming solar panels. Couldn't that have got in here and somehow linked up with the screen?'

'No,' Alan said. 'It was all inhibited. It had rules applied to it. Boundaries, borders and frames. It couldn't migrate from the plantation out there to here. To anywhere.' But even as he said the words Alan was wondering if maybe that was the explanation. He flicked his scanner wand to nano and it came alive with clicks and pulses wherever he pointed it. The room was alive with tech.

'But it's migrated, I gather,' Tier said.

* * *

They locked the door. Tier drove off to his next appointment, but had promised to send some techs out A.S.A.P., except he had pronounced it *a-sap*, and Alan had thought he meant it as an insult. He left instructions for Alan, which basically amounted to mapping the extent of the nanotech migration from the plantation. Tier also told Alan to tell the techs not to mention anything about it to anyone until they'd determined what was really going on. Tier had interests in lots of tech companies and nearly all of them were involved in the application of nanotech in some form. Funnily enough, Tier knew next to nothing about the tech he dealt with. He used to quip that he knew enough to be dangerous but his tech staff had privately argued that he knew so little he was dangerous, and that if ignorance were indeed bliss, then Tier was one very happy guy.

Alan could understand why it might be a good idea to keep this to themselves. People were funny about nanotech and they always worried that it could do all sorts of weird stuff. Alan often found people's ignorance about things that were now a part of everyday life amusing but he put that thought aside as he tried to figure out why this nanotech was doing all sorts of weird stuff. If the prospective buyers found out about the odd goings on, they might not buy the land. Normally this wouldn't have worried Alan overly much but Tier had given him shares in the company in lieu of severance pay. Hopefully they would have days before anyone from the media showed up.

He put the kettle on and made himself a cup of coffee. It was instant. It would have to do. He walked outside and could still see the dust from Tier's car as it made its way down the hill toward the small town of Trafalgar. He looked at the trees. He looked at the power pole that did not have a line to the workshop. He looked at his coffee. Then he looked at the long line of media cars making their way up the hill. Then he looked at the ghost who was walking near the power pole. He would have spent more time wondering about the ghost, but he really wanted to look at the electric kettle and see if he could get it to make another, stronger coffee without power before the media arrived.

'Where are the ghosts?'

'Why are there ghosts?'

'When are they visible?'

'What do the ghosts do?'

Alan was angry at himself for getting flustered when reporters fired this barrage of questions at him and his stupid response had just fired them up even more. Instead of denying any knowledge outright he had asked his own questions back at them.

'Why do you think there are ghosts?' he had asked, which would have been fine except that, before the reporters could answer he had added, 'Who told you about them?' Which simply confirmed, in the reporters' minds, the existence of the Trafalgar Ghosts.

* * *

It turned out that one reporter had been exploring a fairly boring story about a real estate developer paying backhanders to a government official to expedite the sale of some land that had been teched up to add to the town's electricity supplies and someone had mentioned the fact that a few people had claimed to have seen ghosts in and around the area in question.

Alan had sought to downplay the ghost story by scoffing at it.

Tier wouldn't want the ghost story getting out even if it were patently ridiculous. Unfortunately he picked the wrong way to downplay it.

'Ghosts are the least of our problems right now,' he said regretting it even as he said it.

'Why?' the reporters asked. 'What other problems do you have?'

Just then a reporter came out of the workshop. Alan hadn't even seen her go in.

'How come there's nanotech stuff all over the place in here?' she asked as she pointed back within the workshop. 'And how come there's no power hooked up but power's available and why is the word "Do" on a screen in there.'

Why did she have to spout all of that? Alan was confused, angry and a bit out of his depth. Why would a reporter yell all of that out? Why wouldn't she just keep it quiet and ask about it in private instead of telling all of these other reporters about it?

Then he looked at the reporter standing in the doorway and he realised she wasn't a reporter. He had seen her in town. He'd seen her standing in front of signs asking why the town was about to lose their very own electrical supply.

The real reporters all stormed madly into the workshop. When Alan walked in they were grouped around the computer screen.

'What else does it say?' one asked.

'It just says "Do", Alan said.

'Do what?' another asked.

'I don't know,' Alan said and that threw them all into a frenzy of writing on their pads and phones. 'But I'm sure it isn't important,' Alan added.

* * *

The next day, Alan noticed that the word 'Do' had become the slogan for a running shoe company within the day. It was shorter and more to the point than the slogan their competitor used. Two days later the word went viral on the net as a sort of catch all word for positive behaviour. There were educational programs based on the word 'Do' that were being planned as professional development for administrators just days after the report about the computer screen hit the online news services.

* * *

Alan and Tier were back in the workshop along with Tier's senior tech man and his PR person. And there was Dennis Beacham, a reporter who had been elected as the one representative of the media throng that was camped outside of a hastily erected fence. The PR woman was regarding the computer screen with disdain.

'It isn't much to look at is it? Can we make it do other things?'

'Like what?' Alan asked. 'It isn't hooked up to anything, remember? It isn't supposed to be displaying that word. It shouldn't be doing anything.'

'Why "Do" though?' Beacham asked, which was of course what a lot of people were asking. Entire websites had come into existence within weeks of the discovery. There were Facebook pages and 'Do' sites everywhere.

'God knows,' Alan said dismissively and the Church of Positivism was taking donations and receiving tax breaks in less than twenty-four hours.

Tier had ordered his men to strengthen the enclosure around the worksite and had also organised patrols along its length. There was now a small tent city camped on the side of the hill overlooking Trafalgar. Tier kept telling people not to come and, as Alan had quite rightly predicted, they kept coming. Alan couldn't see why Tier was happy about this. Okay, it got the site some good publicity, but it was a hassle dealing with all of the people.

'It's fantastic Alan,' Tier explained. 'Property prices are going through the roof. People love this place. Look at the view,' he said, pointing out of the small caravan window and only seeing tents. 'Do-town! That's what they call it. And I'm a "can do" kinda guy. People are queuing up to buy land and we haven't even cleared it yet.'

Alan's phone had been busy vibrating all morning. He'd stopped answering it simply because he was sick of people asking about the message. That was what it was now, *The* Message. With capital letters. They had also been dealing with requests to see the actual computer screen and people were obsessed with what it might all mean. Alan personally thought it was either a con trick orchestrated by Tier in order to improve the prices of the blocks of land he wanted to sell, or it was a weird electronic glitch. Somehow, some power had somehow been stored in the wires and chips of the computers and the screen... And somehow, that power had manifested itself by lighting up a few pixels on an old Word document. Or something like that. Alan was aware that there were a lot of 'somehows' in the whole thing but he couldn't think of anything else to explain it all. More interesting to him was the appearance of the ghosts.

He had seen them, or had thought he'd seen them, just after the discovery of the word. He was walking up toward the workshop one evening and he saw Kerin Lanley, a reporter, poking around the southern end of the plantation. He called out to her. She just kept walking and then she sort of shimmered, disappeared, and reappeared about three metres away from where Alan was standing. And all of that would have been fine apart from the fact that Kerin was standing beside him at the time.

'Who are you yelling at?' she asked.

'Nothing. No-one,' Alan replied. When 'Kerin' reappeared Alan noticed that she was wearing different clothes to the Kerin beside him. Then the reappearing Kerin disappeared again. That all seemed so long ago now. Alan had seen ghosts of her again, as well as ghosts of Beacham and Tier. He'd even seen ghosts of himself, which had freaked him out a little at the time. The crowds outside the perimeter of the plantation had grown considerably after the news of the ghosts had got out, but it was all strangely quiet now.

* * *

The mist just hung in the still air like spores. This all helped to create the thick stillness that enveloped the plantation toward evening. It would get cooler later on, but it was pleasant as Alan walked from the office block containing the monosyllabic screen to his caravan. He saw a line near the power pole that the techs had erected near the van. The pole was draped in solar cells and enhancers and actually shone with the golden light of the misted sunset. It looked totemic. It also looked symbolic, but Alan couldn't quite figure out what it was symbolic of apart from the obvious. It was only the glowing of the pole that highlighted the slick black protrusion that was within two feet of the base of the pole. Alan didn't know the growth rate of the nanotech installed in the plantation but he didn't think it should have been that quick.

He walked up to the line and examined it. It wasn't growing visibly but he was sure he'd seen it pulse or move. In fact, Alan had a vague feeling that the shiny black tech protrusion was aware of his presence. Tier had been less than diligent in recording the types and nature of the nanotech they'd used in the plantation. Alan had heard of some nanotechs that had a template for self-preservation. This kind of nano could disguise themselves to avoid detection. Others could emit electrical discharges to discourage investigation by animals. Rats loved nanotech. They had devoured it as soon as they found it until the nanotechnicians devised a program that they inserted into a lot of nanotech installations. The rats were devoured by the tech. There was some outcry that this was a bit cruel but by this time nano was a big concern and the companies producing it were able to buy the votes of various political parties. The rats became a part of the system. Some said that there were always rats in the system anyway so it didn't really matter.

Very gently Alan dug around the black, gelatinous tip of the nanoline that was protruding from the red earth like a finger. He set up a small inhibitor that he had found among the tools provided for him when he had first entered the plantation with a view to dismantling the system. This made him think that the nano system in use was bound to have a self-defensive element. They would not have supplied inhibitors if they didn't think he was going to need them. He stepped back and activated the small plastic circle, checked that it was operating and then went back to his van.

* * *

After he'd gone, the nanoline extrusion that had been examining the power pole turned its attention to the inhibitor that Alan had placed around it. All of the mote-like machines within the line began to build and rebuild until they had constructed yet another extension. This extension wavered about some two centimetres above the original black finger-like protrusion, and then it plunged into the inhibitor like a striking snake. The inhibitor and the extension writhed around each other for a moment or two and then sunk into the ground. And there had been no sound at all.

* * *

Alan watched as Tier's car drove up to the gates. He noted that they didn't automatically open as they should have and was not especially surprised. He walked down to the gate. Alan saw another car pull off the road some way behind Tier's car and he was not overly surprised by that either. Alan reached the entrance just as Tier gave up on his remote and had left his car in order to examine the gate controls manually. He did not look up as Alan approached but kept worrying at the gate controls.

'What the hell is the matter with this thing,' he said. Alan assumed it wasn't a question directed to him.

'Well?' Tier said loudly.

'It's probably something to do with the power supply,' Alan said. 'It'd be a good idea to leave your car out there anyway. I'll grab a ladder and you can climb over.'

'I can climb it, I think,' Tier said sardonically. 'Anyway, there isn't a power supply. We agreed not to connect in case it upset the screen.'

'There is a power supply now,' Alan said.

'How do you mean? Have the tech's installed one? It had better be insulated. I don't want anything upsetting that screen.'

'I'll show you,' Alan said.

The two men made their way up a slight incline towards the plantation offices. The office was sited within a natural amphitheatre that protected the buildings from the worst of the wind that swept up the valley but that gave the workers a good view of the valley below.

It was a steep incline in places and Tier was regretting not forcing Alan to bring his car through the gate. He paused a couple of times, ostensibly to look at the view, but he really just wanted to catch his breath. The valley floor was still covered by a morning mist that would soon be burnt off by the sun. And if that didn't happen it would be blown away. Tier could feel the beginnings of a soft breeze at his back as he looked into the mists below.

'What's the problem with bringing a car up here,' he asked.

'The problem is you may not get it back down again,' Alan said.

'Okay,' Tier said. 'Problems then… fixable?'

'I don't know.'

They started walking again. Alan was guiding them so that they would enter the building area from the side of the car park rather than from the rough road from the gate. Tier saw why as soon as they reached the cleared area.

'What the hell is it?' he asked.

'It *was* my power pole,' Alan said. 'I'm not sure what it is now.'

Tier didn't want to get too close and Alan didn't invite him to. There was no need anyway. The pole was now a writhing black mass of nanowires some of which were as thick as a man's wrist. The lines glistened as if they had moisture adhering to them. Tier kept thinking of entwined snakes but forced the image from his mind. This was tech stuff and they had better get a load of techs in to deal with it. He pulled out his phone and Alan quickly slapped it from his hand. Tier shot him a dark look but realised that he must have had a reason. He looked to where his phone had landed. It was already covered by snaking coils of black nanowire. The shape of the phone was still discernible but that was all.

'Shit.'

Both of the men took a step backward.

'That's why it wouldn't have been a good idea to bring your car up,' Alan said. 'As it is it may not be safe where it is. And we need to move people back further.'

'We've moved them back a fair way already. The reporters aren't happy. I don't like reporters who aren't happy. They get all sneaky.'

'Yeah, I know. One followed you up,' Alan said. 'She's just behind those trees over there. I just thought it would be a good idea to make sure she doesn't try to do what you just did or gets her tablet out or something. I don't know what this stuff will do if it gets hold of someone actually using a phone.' He pointed back to where the black mass had consumed the phone. There was now only a writhing mass of glistening black nanowire, slowly sinking into the ground.

'It's obscene,' Tier said. 'Makes me feel a bit sick. They're not supposed to have replicating nanotech up here.'

'I know,' Alan said. 'That's what I was told too. I'm bloody glad I found the screen before I started ripping out the stuff like I was supposed to. God knows what it would have done.'

'You talk like it's smart... like it has a defensive capability or something'

'Well it can acquire. That much is obvious. I imagine something that can acquire like that stuff would be pretty keen to protect its acquisition.'

Tier just nodded. All sorts of things were racing through his mind and the major consideration was getting some tech support to look over the nanotech. It was like no nano he'd seen before.

'Where's that reporter? Are you sure it wasn't a ghost? What the hell is with all that anyway?'

'Over there,' Alan said indicating a pile of broken branches that had been heaped at the edge of the plantation. As he spoke Kerin Lanley meekly rose from behind the dead branches and gave the two men a pathetic little wave. She then started to walk toward them, carefully skirting around the area where the nanowire had appeared.

'Can't say I've ever been followed before,' Tier said. He was scowling. Kerin stood before the two men and pointed to the mass of wires that made up the pole.

'What the hell is that?' she asked.

'It's a—'

'It's a new type of nano product,' Tier interrupted. 'It's secret. It has all sorts of patents out on it and also a lot of commercial confidentiality clauses relating to the intellectual property inherent in it. You may not report it, allude to it or seek any further information about it.'

'You don't know what it is then,' Kerin said. 'It's pretty... energetic isn't it?' The wires were still writhing around each other.

'Where did they come from? What are they doing? Is this something to do with the message on the screen and the ghosts? Do something with these wires? I bet I'm close aren't I?'

'You do pause to draw breath occasionally don't you?' Tier asked.

'I need to get a vid of this,' Kerin said. Tier grabbed her by the elbow. 'Kerin isn't it? Kerin Lanley? Please... I don't that you followed me up here. You know I know your boss. This must remain quiet until my company can figure it out. Now, you're trespassing. I know you think you have a right to tell the world about this but you don't. Now, I'll ensure that whatever our techs find out about this nano stuff, everyone will be informed.'

Kerin looked dubious. 'And will we get access to *all* the information you dig up about this stuff *and* the dead screen scroll.'

Tier frowned. 'Is that what you call it? The message?'

'Someone at the office called it that. The dead screen scrolls. They think it will turn out to be a religious tract or some sort of divinely inspired message.'

'It's a bit slow for a divinely inspired message isn't it?' Alan said. 'It's just been one word for days.'

'That's another thing,' Kerin said. 'Can I get access to the screen at all times? If and/or when another word appears I want to know immediately. And can I have exclusive rights to report it?.'

'How can you have access to it all the time?' Tier asked. 'We can't set up a cam on it. You've seen what happens to tech.'

Alan's attention was drawn by a movement over behind the pile of branches. Kerin Lanley stood up from branches and waved meekly at him. Then, as she began to walk up behind the first Kerin, she began to dissolve. There was a soft hiss as she seemed to disappear in a slow cascade of dust motes.

'I think we need to do something about the ghosts too,' Alan said. As he said it, he noticed a slight change in the glow emanating from the shed. It was somehow brighter.

* * *

Some technicians and PR people were seated with Alan in the small conference room of a local hall. Tier had promised to rent it out for a few days for an incredible amount of money. There were no others present.

'Ghosts, tech, and message,' Tier said. 'There has to be money in this somewhere.' He looked around at the blank faces. 'So what have got?'

Alan waited but no-one seemed to want to talk so he decided he would. 'The second word has thrown a bit of a spanner into the mix. Everyone was expecting "Do good" or "Do unto others", or something like that. "Do not…" implies a longer message.' Alan paused and noticed that all of the PR people were madly making notes and all of the technicians were looking at him expectantly. He pushed on when the pause got too long to bear.

'Many of the churches that sprung up when we just had the word "Do" are having to rewrite their scriptures. The Church of Positivism has become the Church of Positive Negativism. People aren't happy. Half those protestors are people who say we are playing around with their spiritual beliefs.

'A longer message would be a good thing, wouldn't it?' Tier asked enthusiastically. 'A nice long message will keep interest up. More land sales. Hell, more t-shirt sales too. Pity it sounds sort of negative though. Anyway, we have the message. A little bit negative but we can work with it. We have the tech aspect. There's no power source for the computer and any tech that gets too close gets... umm...'

'Eaten?' Alan suggested.

'No. Too negative. And what with the negative message and everything...'

'How about "subsumed",' a PR person said. Tier look unenthused.

'Incorporated?'

'A bit "Trekky" or something,' Tier said.

'Enhanced?' Alan offered.

'How is a piece of tech getting eaten by black slithering nanotech "enhanced" as you call it?' the PR person asked.

'Okay, never mind that. Let's go with enhanced for now,' Tier said. 'Okay so, That's The Message, the tech angle and we also have the ghost bit. What's the go with the ghosts? We know that they aren't really ghosts don't we? That's just a given isn't it?'

There was silence.

'Wow. You mean they really are ghosts?'

Alan said, 'They aren't ghosts in the sense of spirits of people who have died. We are not sure what they are. But they are certainly linked to the tech stuff as they only appear near the source of the tech.'

'So they could be ghosts?' Tier said.

'No,' Alan said. 'They aren't ghosts.'

Tier looked a little deflated. 'But that's not been proven one way or the other,' he said.

A PR person coughed and gave a little embarrassed look around the table and slowly dissolved into a cloud of dust.

* * *

On a trip into town, Tier noticed that the ghosts had begun to turn up all further away from the tech up the hill. People, buildings and even trees occasionally dissolved into tiny motes of dust. He got his tech people looking into it just in case there was some money in it somewhere. The dust was found to be nanotech, which pleased Tier as he thought that bestowed some ownership upon his companies. Sometimes it was dead tech and other times motes formed little galaxies and then coalesced into new people, buildings or whatever. There seemed to be no real guiding intelligence behind the creations. Or at least that was the general opinion until the next word appeared on the screen.

'Do not think.'

Tier looked up from the screen in the shed. 'When did it appear?' he asked.

'About an hour ago,' a technician replied. 'We were just doing the routine checks and there it was.'

'Do not think,' Tier said slowly. 'No, I don't like the sound of that at all. That's way too negative. It hasn't got out yet has it?'

'Not yet but it won't be long,' Alan said. 'You gave that reporter open access remember and she may have seen the new message before we were able to shut it down.'

'Bugga,' Tier said. 'I hate it when I don't feel I have control.'

'And you feel you generally have control of all of this, do you?' Alan asked as he waved his arms around room. 'The message, the tech stuff and the ghosts? I mean, we don't even understand it let alone have control of it. Jesus, have a look around you.'

There was a pause. Then there was a soft hiss. And the desk in front of Alan began to dissolve. Then the walls of the shed became opaque and finally fell away in clouds of dust motes. Alan began to panic as everything around him shifted and dissolved. He looked at Tier's panic-stricken face and was almost relieved to know that he was not the only one experiencing this phenomenon. Then, without warning, the room and desks all became solid again.

Alan and Tier glanced at each other.

'Did you see that?' Tier asked.

'Yes,' Alan said. 'Did I disappear?'

'Yes,' said Tier. 'Did I?'

Alan said, 'It's sort of like everything has been remade in nanotech.'

'Everything? You really think that?' Tier said and Alan noted the fear in his voice.

There was silence between the two men. Alan looked out of the window at the forest. It shimmered and Alan found it hard to actually focus on the individual trees. He turned his attention to the hills and the town beyond and had the same problem. Alan felt some sort of vertigo and realised that this must be how people felt during earthquakes when they lost confidence in the earth.

Alan's reverie was interrupted by Tier.

'So, are we real? I feel real. Do you feel real?'

'I'm not sure how I feel,' Alan said. He looked down at the screen with the single word 'Do' shimmering faintly.

'Do not think for a minute that I am happy about this,' Tier said. 'I'm supposed to be on a flight for a meeting.'

Alan checked the comp again. There was definitely no power connected to it. He had a thorough rummage around the back of the comp and ensured that there were no leads at all. There wasn't. There weren't even any unplugged leads.

'Nothing,' he said.

'There must be something,' Tier replied.

The Author: Stephen Higgins

Stephen helped to get *Aurealis* off the ground and is inordinately proud of all that it has achieved. He has had a few stories published and the odd play performed. He currently teaches English and Media at Trafalgar High School in Gippsland, Victoria, Australia. He plays guitar well enough to amuse himself and annoy others. He has been reading speculative fiction for an awfully long time and he still loves it.

Story Behind the Story

'Forest/Trees' started life as a small idea about a pine forest that was being fed nutrients via a plastic tube watering system. I was installing a watering system at home at the time. I had the initial idea of the delivery system being made of nanotechnology and the trees being enhanced by 'nanotech' to improve their growth. I guess it's an environmental story basically. That original concept grew into a bloated story that tried to include far too many elements in the hope of it forming the basis of a novel. Fortunately, I decided to pare it back to the basic story and allow it grow naturally. This is what it became.

The Illustrator: Lynette Watters

Lynette hails from the wild outer west of Sydney. She enjoys reading ancient science fiction, drawing imaginary dreamscapes and naked people, designing massive dreamhouses and procrastinating. Her ideal job would allow her to enjoy all of these things and still allow her to sleep in.

Illustration by Kim Lennard

Mayfire

Rebecca Birch

Eilis huddled in the last thin beam of daylight angling through the window of her father's cottage, feverishly working the shuttle of her lap-loom with trembling hands.

'You'll not finish the May ribbon before tomorrow, Eilis,' her father, Henrick, said. He reclined in a rocking chair of shaped beech, puffing from a long pipe. The smoke curled toward the roof to join the cloud that formed there every night, pungent and stifling. 'You failed last year and the year before. Why would this year be different?'

Eilis bit the inside of her cheek. She wouldn't take his bait. If she spent her energy on arguing, then he'd be right. The sun would rise on the first day of May and, once more, she would be without a ribbon to join in the dance. Sentenced to another year of maidenhood and no hope of a reprieve from her father's dark moods and sharp tongue.

'Did you hear me, girl?'

She sighed and lifted up the loom's shed. 'Yes, Father.'

'I'll not have you keeping the fire going all night long, either,' he said. 'Waste of fuel. It goes out when I'm through with it.'

The westering sun slipped lower, shrinking the beam of daylight. Eilis readjusted her position and re-threaded the shuttle. Only an inch left to go. Only an inch. She repeated the words in her mind with each sweep. Only an inch.

She should have been imbuing prayers into the weave, like the night when she'd dyed the threads with woad under the first full moon after midwinter by the bank of the Long River—a maiden's prayers for a good man. A strong defender, successful provider, and, that most elusive of dreams, a man she could love, and would give her the same in return.

With her father's sharp stare burning into her back, she couldn't. The sole prayer she had room for was *'only an inch'*. An inch to begin her own life. It didn't matter if she found a defender, or provider, or even a lover.

The waning sun glinted off the silver wire, so thin it bent and flowed like thread, which she had woven through the ribbon's deep blue expanse, calling to mind the stars that dotted the night sky like spilled salt.

The *creak-thump* of her father's rocker picked up tempo and he began to hum a tuneless melody, just off the beat. He knew his singing drove her to distraction.

Eilis picked up the silver-threaded shuttle and slid it through the warp threads too hard. Too fast. The wire caught her finger, biting sharp and deep.

Hissing in a breath, she shoved the injured finger into her mouth and pressed her tongue against the wound. The warm, metallic taste of her blood settled at the junction between her throat and the base of her nose. Her finger throbbed.

Eilis pushed the loom aside and reached for her sewing box. A few scraps of old linen sat in the bottom corner. She pulled them out and tied one around the tip of her finger, pressing hard. Blood seeped into the cloth in a spreading stain. Another rag, and another. The last remained white, at least for the moment. It would have to do.

She pulled the loom back into place. A drop of blackness darkened the cloth where she had bled onto the ribbon. Her heart thudded like her father's mallet against his square carpenter's nails when the bleak moments hit him. Hard and wild.

Eilis dabbed at the spot, her teeth sharp against her lower lip, but the blood would not come clean. It clung to the fibres as if it were a part of the dye.

May ribbons were supposed to be perfect. No blemish. Nothing save the threads and the maiden's prayers or the magic might fail to kindle the Mayfire—the consuming flame that guided young women along the path from maidenhood to wife.

Eilis's jaws tightened until pain flared where she bit her lip. The woad's deep blue, the colour of twilight, nearly hid the stain. Maybe the priests wouldn't see it. Maybe if she could only complete the weaving and present her first ribbon they would overlook the error. It was only a small stain. Surely it wouldn't break the spell she'd worked so hard to weave.

She ignored the small voice at the back of her mind that reminded her of the few maidens who had perished in the rite. If the Mayfire did not find its release, it burned the maidens from the inside out. It didn't matter. That hadn't happened since Eilis was a wee thing. Besides, she couldn't give up. Not now.

With trembling hands, she slid the silver thread back and took up the other shuttle. The sunbeam narrowed to a sliver of gold. Dust motes hung in the air like a cloud of stars. They dimmed and vanished into invisibility with the falling of night.

Eilis gathered her sewing box, loom, and wrapped shuttles, uncrossed her legs, and moved unsteadily toward the hearth, sharp needles stabbing her from thighs to toes.

The moment she knelt to begin her work again in the fickle firelight, her father rose and stretched. His shoulder popped. 'Time for bed,' he said. 'Put out the fire.'

Frustrated tears pricked at the back of Eilis's eyelids. Her chest constricted. 'Please, Father. It's so close. Just a little longer and I'll be done.'

It galled her to beg. Her stomach felt sick, and she blinked at the stinging sensation burning her eyes. She wouldn't cry. Not in front of him.

'This is my house. These are my rules.' Henrick shoved her sewing box aside with the toe of his boot and kicked the bucket of sand at the side of the hearth. 'Put it out.'

Eilis obeyed. She scattered the sand with numb hands and watched the logs sputter and fizzle. It was too easy to imagine those dying flames as the extinguishing of her dreams. Her face burned with smothered anger and frustration.

When the fire lay dead her father cleared his throat. 'I know you wanted it, Eilis,' he said in a gruff voice, 'but this is for the best.'

'The best for who?' She couldn't keep the words contained.

His heavy hand rested on her shoulder. 'It's over. Let it go.'

Eilis swallowed a response. It would only break on the lump that clogged her throat, making her sound weak. A weak woman would never complete a May ribbon. A weak woman didn't deserve the reward that waited beyond.

After a moment, her father pulled his hand away and clomped across the floorboards to the window. He closed and bolted the shutters. The room fell into blackness. 'We'll go to the May field with the sunrise. See the ribbons and the dance. Maclin said he and Hamish would be there. We'll join them, you and me. Together. Just the way it should be.'

His footsteps moved to his room and the door closed behind him with a solid thud.

Eilis cradled her head in her hands. Her breath heated the air. The injured finger throbbed with the pulse of her heart. It would be so easy to surrender, to admit she would never finish a May ribbon. Not with her father's constant intervention.

What would her mother, Maeve, have said had she still lived? To give up? To be happy with her lot? Forever a maiden, forever trapped to live at her father's whims?

Eilis didn't think so. She drew the memory of her mother's face to the back of her eyelids and studied it. Maeve's pale skin, much like her own, dotted with freckles, wide blue eyes that never seemed to see the darkness of the world, only the small joys hidden beneath the surface—the springing of the first tendrils of the strawberry vines, or the *rat-tat-tat* of a woodpecker's drum, signalling the coming of the springtime.

Maeve had taken the world and turned it over like a plough, making everything new and vital. She had completed her own ribbon. Her marriage to Eilis's father was proof of it.

Eilis tried to see the world with her mother's innocent beliefs that there was good to be found in everything, but since the fever had stolen Maeve away five years past, it was hard. Too hard. Henrick hadn't been so callous then, while Maeve was among the living. What sort of world would tear the heart from a man? From a daughter now left to fill a void too large for her small strength?

Was it easier for men? Maclin had lost his own wife many years ago, leaving him to raise Hamish alone, but he bore it more easily than Henrick. The anger that simmered beneath Henrick's skin, ready to boil over, didn't touch Maclin.

Hamish must be a better son than Eilis was a daughter. He was always there when Maclin came calling, quiet and watchful, his gaze intent beneath prominent dark eyebrows. They'd been there earlier in the evening, talking, while she wove in the corner.

Her thoughts back to the present, Eilis fumbled for the loom. Finding its rigid end, she pulled it close and squinted. If she could see just a little she could keep trying, but the darkness was complete.

Rat–tat–tat.

Eilis froze, her breath caught in mid-inhale.

Rat–tat–tat.

It was too late for woodpeckers. They wouldn't fly in darkness. Eilis surged to her feet. If the moon gave enough light for a woodpecker, it would be enough for her purposes.

She gathered her things. Her arms and legs trembled, making it difficult to move in silence. Her father wouldn't approve—he'd try to stop her if he heard—but he hadn't forbidden her to go outside. This one time, she would make her own choice and brave the consequences.

Eilis pressed open the front door, dreading the creak she knew would come when it passed the sticky spot in the hinges, and winced when it came. Motionless, she waited, all her senses trained on her father's door.

Nothing.

Letting out her breath, she slipped through the front door into the soft blue light of the crescent moon and followed the path to the bank of the Long River. Settling herself by the shore, she slipped out the shuttles and began to weave. It felt right to be there, in the same place she'd begun the work so many months ago. Up and down went the warp threads, back and forth the weft, dancing in tempo with the babble of the water and the woodpecker's steady *rat–tat–tat.*

***

Tap–tap–tap, came a rap at Eilis's bedchamber door. 'Time to be up, girl.'

Her eyes fluttered open. Sticky sleep clung in the edges. She felt as if she'd only just fallen into slumber, but when her fingers closed on the folded ribbon in her right hand, a rush of energy washed through her, dashing away the clinging webs of weariness.

'I'm coming, Father.'

She rose and splashed her face with cool water from the basin atop her cupboard. Opening the cupboard door, she touched the pure white fabric of the May kirtle hanging there, as it had for three years, untouched. Never before had she earned the right to don it. Now she held the finished ribbon, but knew that if she wore the kirtle, her father would find a way to forbid her from attending the rites.

There was little to be done. A maiden must wear the kirtle, so she slipped it over her head. The fabric was tight across her breasts—it had been made when she was not yet so fully matured—but the seams held. Over it, she donned a simple muslin day dress that hid the kirtle fully, save when she walked. Flashes of the white fabric beneath flashed if she moved too quickly.

Reminding herself to go slow, Eilis slipped the completed ribbon into a deep pocket of the day dress, gathered her heavy black curls into a loose braid, and tied it off with a green cord.

She opened the door. 'I'm ready.'

* * *

Celebrants dotted the May field like wildflowers. Little girls in bright colours, boys wearing dyed-wool felt hats, the priests and maidens in brilliant white. Hopeful young men—and some not so young—gathered in clusters, marked by their stark black festival robes. They carried flower chaplets, some holding them loose and swaying at their sides, others clinging to the delicate blooms with both hands so hard they crushed the petals beneath their fingers.

'Not many maidens this year,' her father said.

'Too few for all the men,' Eilis replied. It was ever the case. The priests claimed it made those men who were gifted with wives more likely to honour them.

'Look, Father, there's Maclin by the ale-cart.' She pointed to her father's boyhood friend. 'Why don't you go and share a mug?'

Her father cast the cart and Maclin a longing look. 'You'll be all right?'

'I'll be fine. Go on. Enjoy the Maying.'

She watched him until he had his own mugful of the dark amber ale that the brewmistress made special for the Maying each year. When he was fully occupied, Eilis slipped down the gentle slope of the green toward the circle of priests.

They stood apart from the rest, gathered in conversation with the maidens. Eilis touched the elbow of Kirkan, one of the most senior priests—the one who had conducted the rites when Maeve's body was turned to flame and became part of the breath of the world.

Kirkan turned away from the others, regarding her with a steady gaze. 'What is it, Eilis?'

'I've come to present myself as a maiden.'

'You have no kirtle.'

'Yes,' she said, lifting the hem of her day dress to show the white beneath, 'I do. And I have a ribbon.'

She slipped the long ribbon out of her pocket and held it out to the priest.

Kirkan took it, his age-withered hands showing no tremor. Slowly, he pulled the length of it between his fingers, studying the weave. 'Why did you choose woad?' he asked. 'Its cost is dear, and there are other colours more suited to Maying than twilight.'

Eilis looked down at her hands. 'It felt right. Listen to the breath of the world and it will guide you to the true nature of your heart. That's what you've always told us.'

Kirkan ran his finger down the fabric. 'Dark and shadowed, but knit through with hidden strength. I think you've chosen rightly.' He paused, his finger hovering over the dark spot where her blood had fallen the night before. His eyes flashed from the stain to her bandaged finger and back again to her face.

Eilis drew in a breath, straightened her shoulders, and tilted up her chin, returning the priest's stare with one of her own. Let him see she wasn't afraid. Let him see how much this meant. Surely he couldn't turn her away. Not after all this time.

His lips pressed into thin lines and a deep wrinkle creased along his jaw. 'How many years has it been since your mother died?'

'Five.'

'Does your father know you've finished this?'

Eilis gave a sharp shake of her head. 'No.' She could have said more. That she feared he'd keep her from the rites. That she couldn't bear to stay bound in his joyless house. That without her mother's bright smile and easy laugh, the only thing holding her together was the dream of forging a new life for herself. A new life on her own terms.

She said none of those things. Kirkan would accept her offering or not on its own merits. The muscles at the base of her neck clenched and her hands, empty now, ached for something to hold on to.

Kirkan hesitated, running his finger over the bloodstain, his eyes distant. 'Very well,' he said at last. 'Go and join the maidens. And take off your outer dress. If you're to be a maiden, you will do it fully.'

Eilis's knees went weak and her breath rushed out so fast it set her head spinning. 'Thank you, Kirkan. Thank you.'

He handed back her ribbon and waved her toward the cluster of maidens. 'Go.'

* * *

Eilis stood at the base of the Maypole, one of only eight maidens, shining white against the green. Her long hair now draped freely, thick curls licking around her face in the wind. Her ribbon hung from the circle at the Maypole's crest—a single thin strip of the night sky in a field of gold, pink, red, and green. She didn't regret her choice. It might not be a traditional colour of the Maying, but it was hers, and it spoke her true nature.

The hopeful men, found to be worthy by right of their work and their deeds, ringed around them. A full twenty this year. Some younger than herself, some nearly as old as her father, some bachelors, some widowers, all dreaming of a life partner. A helpmate and guide.

Eilis didn't look at their faces, staring instead at their robes, blowing gently in the breeze. Most of them she knew, at least a bit, despite how little time she'd spent among them since Maeve's death. She wouldn't torment herself now with wondering who the ribbon might choose for her. Better not to know.

A frisson of nerves shuddered down her spine. Had she prayed hard enough while she wove? How many times had she been distracted? Wishing more for an escape than for a true partner? How much of that had transferred itself into her weaving?

The musicians began to play, a haunting modal melody, beginning with a single reed flute, then adding in a vielle, a lute, the drums. The beat seeped into her skin, urging her feet to dance. As one, the maidens took the dangling ends of their ribbons in their hands.

They faced opposite each other in pairs. Eilis's gaze met with the woman in front of her, a flame-haired beauty, her cheeks flushed with excitement. Every man present would be watching this one, praying that she would be the fulfilment of their desires. Who would look at poor, simple Eilis? A dark-haired, dainty thing. The sorrowful daughter of a lost man.

She closed her eyes and waited for the cue to begin the dance. It came when the melody swirled to a crescendo then dropped into silence, leaving the field in an expectant hush.

'Eilis!' Henrick's shout ripped through the quiet.

She flinched. *Not now. Please, don't try to stop me now.*

The musicians ignored his shout and picked up the tune again at a pulsing tempo. Eilis's feet moved without thought. Forward, beneath her partner's upraised arm, then out while raising her own hand for the next girl to pass beneath.

'Eilis!' The bellow bounced off the walls of her skull.

She closed her eyes and danced on. Her body knew its work without the need of sight. Up, down. Up, down.

Her ribbon warmed, sending heat sliding up her arm. Her eyes flashed open and she glanced at the strip of cloth, woven by her own skill. It glowed with a pale white light, webbed with the other ribbons around the Maypole, each of them shining with their own unique hue. The magic was working. The bloodstain hadn't broken the spell.

'Let me go, you bastard! That's my daughter. Let me pass!'

Unable to ignore the tumult, Eilis looked toward her father's voice. He wrestled with one of the black clad men in the ring of hopefuls. The Mayfire had begun to blur Eilis's vision, but she could see the man was taller than her father, and stronger, too, from the breadth of his shoulders. He dug in his legs and pushed back, an unmovable stone.

The ribbon's heat intensified, so hot it hurt to keep her grip. With a flourish, the flute led the musicians to a faster tempo. Eilis's feet kept pace. Her breath grew shallow. Motes of light drifted up from the ribbons and rained down on the maidens, tingling with energy where they touched skin, mottling the kirtles in all the colours of the rainbow.

'Eilis, you can't do this.' Desperation hollowed out her father's voice, leaving it resonant as a dead tree that had lost its heartwood. 'You can't abandon me like your mother did. Don't leave me alone.' The last word hitched on a strangled sob.

Eilis glanced back in time to see her father collapse. The man he'd been wrestling with caught Henrick as he fell and lowered him to the ground.

Eilis's steps slowed, faltered. Her body ached, a kindled fire raging within. The ribbon was gone, leaving her filled with the Mayfire, limned with white light that shone from her skin.

The music drove to a crescendo and died away into nothingness. Now was the time to close her eyes and let the work of her hands and her heart guide her to her new life.

She couldn't do it.

Her father lay lifeless, his face devoid of colour. Maybe dead. Somewhere nearby a woodpecker set up its pounding.

Eilis staggered across the open green, only vaguely aware of the other maidens making their blind way along the cords of magic that drew them to their destined partners.

The grass beneath her bare feet felt cold and sharp. She'd made the wrong choice. This was her punishment. To fail to find a husband, and lose a father in the same sweep.

She fell to her knees at Henrick's side, her tears turning to steam when they rolled onto her cheeks. How could she have failed so utterly? If Maeve were watching her now, what a disappointment she must find her daughter to be.

Agony seared through her, burning at her heart, flaming in her eyes, tearing at her hands. She reached for her father.

Strong hands grabbed her shoulders. 'He's alive, Eilis. He's alive.'

Eilis tried to shake free of the hands, but the fingers dug into her arms, refusing to release her.

'Let me go.' She hardly recognised her own voice. It sounded as if it came from a great distance, swept away by the firestorm that raged through her.

'No. I won't.'

'*Please.*'

The hands pulled her back, replaced by arms wrapped around her fully, holding her against a firm chest. 'You can't touch him. Not with the fire on you.'

She struggled, fought his iron grip until her strength failed and she hung limp over the man's arm.

'Eilis,' his voice beside her ear was low and urgent, laced with a tracing of pain, 'I promise you he lives, but you must finish the rite, or the fire will consume you and he'll find nothing left but ashes when he wakes.'

She could hardly think. Hardly breathe. All was worry and weariness and throbbing heat.

'Promise that if I let you go, you won't touch him.'

Eilis nodded.

The arms slowly released. Eilis's eyes slipped closed. Her heart raced, fluttering like a bird's. She tried to focus, to slow her breathing, to listen to the breath of the world, but there was nothing. No soft pull to lead her in any direction.

Something had gone wrong. The ribbon's spell fuelled her, but only with fire, not with guidance.

Her blood felt as if it were turning to steam. The wound on her finger lanced her with pain.

The wound. The blood.

It must have changed the spell. It hadn't been worked solely of her dreams and prayers. It wouldn't make her choice for her. She would have to make it for herself, and soon. Her strength faded in the haze of pain and the dizzying rush of her fevered brain.

The man who held her had stopped Henrick from disrupting the rite.

He'd kept her from touching him when the fire would have consumed them both. She did not know the man, but she knew these choices, and she respected them.

Gathering what little strength she had left, Eilis rolled to her side and groped for the man's bare hand. Her fingers caught in his and clutched him like a strong branch in the river. The pain dimmed. His breath hissed in through his teeth and she leaned toward the sound.

When she found his mouth, she hesitated only a moment before touching her lips to his. The Mayfire raced through her, dancing between them like lightning, then ebbing until it transformed into a barely perceptible thread that would never fade.

Eilis's strength faltered. The Mayfire's rush left her weary and weak. The man's arm tightened around her, supporting her, his thumb sliding up and down against her side, soothing and sweet.

She broke away from the kiss first, and blinked up at him, his features registering for the first time. Dark hair with a sharp, hawk-like nose. Blue eyes she'd seen so often before, watching her about her work while their fathers talked and idled. 'Hamish?'

Maclin's son smiled down at her, a look of wonder softening his hard-edged features. He released her hand long enough to settle a flower chaplet atop her head, sealing the rite. 'I knew you'd finish the ribbon this year, Eilis, so I chose to stand, but I could hardly dare to dream that the world would gift me so.'

Eilis smiled tiredly up at him. This quiet, steady man had faith in her, even when she'd doubted herself. It hardly seemed possible.

Then she remembered Henrick. She pulled away from Hamish's embrace and knelt over her father. Now that the Mayfire's haze had lifted, she could see the slow rise and fall of his breathing. Hamish had spoken the truth. Her father lived.

She bent forward until her forehead rested on Henrick's shoulder. He groaned and groped for Eilis's hand. She straightened and grasped his callused fingers. The eyes that blinked up from his pale face somehow reminded Eilis of a lost child, despite the lines that creased his skin.

The thread of magic binding her to Hamish pulsed at the base of her awareness. So new, yet without it she'd feel as if a part of her had been cut off. So it must be for her father. The resentment she'd clung to for those five years while he fell into despondency faded, replaced with a new understanding for all that he had lost.

Hamish touched the small of her back. 'He won't be alone, you know. We'll stay close. Watch over him. Father will help. He's been worried sick since Henrick lost Maeve.'

Eilis looked over her shoulder at her new husband. 'You'd do that for me?'

'For both of you.'

The corner of Eilis's lip twitched into a half-smile. 'I always knew you were a good man. Thank you.'

'I love you, Eilis. Have for years. All I wanted was to find a way to make you smile again.'

A stiff breeze blew past, and for a moment Eilis thought she heard her mother's voice. *Well done, my child. Well done.*

Relief and joy swept through Eilis. The risk had been worth the reward. Together, she and Hamish would build a new life. A happy life. A life built on love for the future and support for the past.

In that moment, Eilis knew her time in the twilight had ended. It was time to walk in the sun.

The Author: Rebecca Birch

Rebecca Birch is a science fiction and fantasy writer based in Seattle, Washington. She's a classically trained soprano, holds a deputy black belt in Tae Kwon Do, and enjoys spending time in the company of trees. Her fiction has appeared in markets including *Nature*, *Cricket*, and *Orson Scott Card's Intergalactic Medicine Show*. She is also a two-time finalist in the Writers of the Future contest. You can find her online at wordsofbirch.com.

Story Behind the Story

When I was younger, I spent many years working as a musician at a medieval faire. Every May we would set up the Maypole, gather the visitors, and lead them in the dance. This image has always stuck with me, and decided I wanted to work it into a story. The weaving of the ribbon as a sort of rite of passage came upon me unexpected, and those two ideas together were the genesis of 'Mayfire'.

Family, duty, independence, and love are themes I have come back to many times. I enjoyed the opportunity to weave them together, much as Eilis weaves her own threads. In the finished product is where the magic lies.

The Illustrator: Kim Lennard

Kim Lennard is a freelance digital artist who has a love for all forms of artwork especially fantasy art. Kim creates her images using a combination of photos, textures and digital painting with Photoshop CS6 and an intuous5 tablet. Kim lives in Newcastle, Australia and undertakes commission artworks for both the literature and music industry. Kim is known as kimsol in the deviantART community and can be contacted there directly at kimsol.deviantart.com.

Robotics, AI and the Impending Techno-Apocalypse

Terry Wood

'The first ultraintelligent machine is the last invention that man need ever make, provided that the machine is docile enough to tell us how to keep it under control.' – JJ Good (1965)

In the popular Terminator series of films, an unsuspecting human military complex builds Skynet, a worldwide defence system, that becomes 'self-aware' and which proceeds to wage war on humanity.

Tony Stark takes a piece of alien technology to develop his 'ultimate' artificial intelligence program 'Ultron'—a global peacekeeping initiative—which builds its own physical form and proceeds to deliver 'peace in our time' by destroying the world.

In *Demon Seed* (1973), Proteus seeks to replicate itself in human form by devising a way to impregnate a female human.

HAL 9000 tries to kill its crew on the *Discovery One*, determined to fulfil its programming.

And the list goes on. Science fiction has already glimpsed the future of a world dominated by powerful computers and robots and the future looks bleak.

Humans seek to develop ever more powerful computers that exceed the capacity of ordinary humans, thinking deeper, faster and without any apparent ethical limits. So, what is the future really going to provide? Will the predictions of SF writers come true (knowing that SF writers are notoriously bad at predicting the future) and will we, as a civilisation, actually do anything about it?

Much has been written about the possible consequences of a world dominated by technology. The loss of jobs and meaningful work raises concerns about the unequal flow of economic benefits that may derive from a world run by big corporations that dominate governments, not from the technology itself, but the resulting concentration of economic wealth in private hands. This is already underway.

Robots—machines that look like a human being and perform the various complex acts of a human being—are one of the mainstream tropes of science fiction. 'Robot' was first coined by Karel Capek in 1920 in his play *R U R*. Robots turning on their creators soon became a common theme, leading Issac Asimov (1950) to develop his famous Three Laws:

A robot may not injure a human being or, through inaction, allow a human being to come to harm.

A robot must obey the orders given it by human beings except where such orders would conflict with the First Law.

A robot must protect its own existence as long as such protection does not conflict with the First or Second Laws.

Robotics is surely a good thing. Allowing boring repetitive work to be done by a machine, faster, more accurately, and longer than any human could hope to achieve, leaving people to spend more time to pursue leisure, culture, art, travel and adventure. A utopia of gleaming driverless cars ready to take you where you want. Automated farms planting and harvesting, linked into a global network to ensure under- and over-supply is a thing of the past. Medical facilities that diagnose ailments and perform complex operations without fault.

Of course, only if it were this simple. Asimov was even compelled to later modify the Three Laws, but to no avail as SF writer Robert J Sawyer (1991) points out:

'We already live in a world in which Asimov's Three Laws of Robotics have no validity, a world in which every single computer user is exposed to radiation that is considered at least potentially harmful, a world in which machines replace people in the workplace all the time. (Asimov's First Law would prevent that: taking away someone's job absolutely is harm in the Asimovian sense, and therefore a "Three Laws" robot could *never* do that, but, of course, real robots do it all the time.)'

Modern day robots have been designed to do manual tasks or solve complex mathematical problems, build cars on an assembly line, or play games using the ability to learn from each game played. Deep Blue and AlphaGo, are now superior to any human grandmaster. But this is still just superior computing power, not 'consciousness', and still requiring humans to tell the machine what to do and when. It will be the drive for better military applications—drones, autonomous weapons systems, remote bomb disposal—that will probably see the fastest developments in robotics. Without war we may not have gotten to the nuclear age so quickly and so, the first AI will likely have guns.

A machine that performs a set of difficult tasks is limited, and requires constant human input. Logic dictates that a machine that 'thinks' for itself would provide even greater benefits. Such a machine with true Artificial Intelligence (AI) is yet to be defined, but, according to Nick Bostrom, should at least feature the capacity to learn and 'to deal effectively with uncertainty and probabilistic information. Some faculty for extracting useful concepts from sensory data and internal states, and for leveraging acquired concepts into flexible combinatorial representations for use in logical and intuitive reasoning…' And it may also have to be able to evolve and therefore be able to reproduce.

But are robots simply to be modern era slaves, subject to the whim of humanity? It does seem logical that a robot with artificial intelligence truly given free will, would soon begin to question its existence and the way it is being treated. Indeed, the question of whether robots should be 'taxed' has already been raised by Bill Gates. Maybe they will need to be paid wages as well.

It's easy for us to forget that robots are not human, but merely designed to replicate tasks performed by humans. But much SF is written giving robots human behaviours, emotions and motivations. A robot that simply always does what it's told and never questions anything, is not going to make much of a plot. Even Data from *Star Trek* gets into all sorts of trouble for wanting to be more 'human' or to understand humans better. This makes sense, of course, if he is to interact meaningfully and successfully with his crewmates.

One the best recent examples of robotics in fiction is Christopher Nolan's *Interstellar* (2014), where TARS and CASE are the nicest robotic assistants you could hope for: polite, efficient, thoughtful and even cheeky. But they both take the shape of a rectangular box, albeit one that can change shape to meet particular limited functions. The only humanoid aspect of these machines is their 'personality'. And, of course, we warm to them in a way that poor HAL could never achieve with its single 'eye' and monotone voice that could not even change as it was being slowly terminated by Dave Bowman.

Of course, androids and cyborgs that blur the line between mechanical being and human make for good storytelling. Ash, Bishop and David from the Alien franchise are great examples of robots that appear more human than machine, but are still programmed for specific purposes, no matter what—and mostly sinister. What is a robot boy to do, once rejected by his human mother, and all he knows and wants is her love? Does he naturally get violent and lash out because of this rejection, or does he just keep looking forever, because that's what his programming tells him to do (*AI Artificial Intelligence*, 2001)?

It is the obsession in 'humanising' robots that makes us uneasy. *Westworld* (1973) and *Blade Runner* (1982) both examine a time when you're not going to quite be sure who you're talking to and whether or not they're going to kill you, just because they can. Robots dissatisfied with their lot, unhappy with what they've been dealt by their creators, wanting a better life, perhaps reflect the human condition more than most. Roy Batty, played menacingly by Rutger Hauer, best illustrates this by telling his 'creator' Eldon Tyrell, 'I want more life, fucker,' just before he kills him.

So, given all that is written warning humanity of the dangers of AI and robots, why do we still proceed to develop this technology?

Jared Diamond best explains this phenomenon in his book *Collapse* (2005), which explores why civilisations come to an end, often not by some cataclysmic event, but a creeping problem that is repeatedly ignored, and the danger grows bit by bit. Every new advancement in AI or robotics may well be heralded as the next positive step, until suddenly it's too late.

But we proceed, because it's going to make our lives easier, healthier, wealthier and happier. And it has and will continue to do so for a while yet. Industrial applications are obvious, but where else: military, law enforcement, emergency search and rescue, medical diagnosis, maybe even sporting teams.

But all is not lost as we prepare to fight against the impending techno-apocalypse.

In 2016, Google, Facebook, Amazon, IBM and Microsoft announced the creation of the *Partnership on Artificial Intelligence to Benefit People and Society* to 'conduct research, recommend best practices, and publish research under an open license in areas such as ethics, fairness and inclusivity; transparency, privacy, and interoperability; collaboration between people and AI systems; and the trustworthiness, reliability and robustness of the technology.' Elsewhere, the *Centre for Human-Compatible Artificial Intelligence* has been launched to ensure an AI doesn't inadvertently harm humans by trying to best fulfil its programming (e.g., start a war to ensure the best possible value for defence bonds or some other futures investment).

So maybe, people are starting to take notice of SF writers, but if history tells us anything, that may not mean much. Robert J Sawyer (1991) again:

'The development of AI is a business, and businesses are notoriously uninterested in fundamental safeguards—*especially* philosophic ones. (A few quick examples: the tobacco industry, the automotive industry, the nuclear industry. Not one of these has said from the outset that fundamental safeguards are necessary, every one of them has resisted externally imposed safeguards, and none have accepted an absolute edict against ever causing harm to humans.)'

Remember, robots are merely tools that may look human-like and are designed to perform human activities. Should a robot care what effects its actions have on the people around it, so long as it is doing what is required? Why should it want to be more human, anyway? The ultimate responsibility falls on humanity to show restraint. Future governments may well outlaw AI development that is not sanctioned by the UN, for example, much like the current nuclear Non-Proliferation Treaty provides for. The international community may well deliver the answer to ensuring AIs have no capacity to do harm. It's a fine line that is drawn between a superintelligence serving humanity and a machine that mimics a human brain and exercises free will.

Homo sapiens is unique among Earth's animal species in its ability to adapt to differing environments and situations, not by evolutionary means—by manipulating its DNA—but by its ability to reason, to work in groups, to evolve culturally. According to Yuval Noah Harari, this 'cognitive revolution' is what allowed *sapiens* to emerge victorious over other humans who existed along with them 150,000 years ago. So now, we are evolving through the fast pace of technological and cultural change, rather than waiting for our DNA to catch up.

An AI, given this same 'cognitive' ability, may ultimately resolve that the next evolutionary phase is to be done with humanity in favour of something better. Perhaps by duplicating itself, or perhaps, by realising that dolphins will make better stewards of the Planet Earth than us.

We still have much to learn about the functioning of the human brain and the nature of consciousness. Perhaps the fact that the human brain misfires quite regularly and is able to produce sociopaths and other abnormal outcomes, both through genetic and environmental causes, means trying to duplicate the brain by means of developing an artificial intelligence is not really the way to go. Maybe more sophisticated robots will be okay, depending on how advanced they are and by grabbing the best bits about the human brain and ignoring the imperfections, if that is even possible.

But all of this may not come to pass. We only need to look to the development of the internet to see what might become of the robotic revolution. Despite the internet's great benefits, one of the largest single uses is to access pornographic and dating sites. Sex sells, and robotics should be no different. Sex robots (like Gigilo Joe), instead of sex dolls? Why not? You'd have to rate this as a certainty and *Ex Machina* (2015) has already shown us how that's going to work out.

Imagine a world where your ideal partner in life is a robot, providing you with everything you need to validate your unique human insecurities and faults. This may well be the greatest threat to humanity—a world where human interaction is replaced by a human-robot world free of the uncertainty of love.

So, do we need to worry about the impending techno-apocalypse, where robots take over the world? Probably not. Our demise may be by something more sinister—our own desires.

The Author: Terry Wood

Terry Wood is a political consultant, writer and editor from Brisbane, Australia. Naturally, the politics and societies of the future, both utopian and dystopian, interest him. He provides editorial support to both *Aurealis* and *Andromeda Spaceways Magazine*, and is still trying to find more time to write fiction.

The History and Future of *Aurealis*
An Interview with Dirk Strasser

Chris Large

Dirk Strasser co-founded Aurealis magazine in 1990 with Stephen Higgins and five years later set up the Aurealis Awards. He's seen Aurealis grow from an idea into the most recognisable name in Australian fantasy and science fiction. As part of the magazine's landmark hundredth issue celebration, he speaks to Chris Large about the past twenty-seven years and beyond of sweat, tears, speculation, and fiction.

Dirk, you've revealed in other forums that when you began *Aurealis* with Stephen Higgins back in 1990, you were readers and would-be writers of SF, but you weren't fans, and didn't really understand fandom. How were you able to produce a magazine that has clearly lasted the test of time?

We learned about fandom pretty quickly. We went from zero awareness of it, to knowing a lot of the main players. In terms of why *Aurealis* has lasted so long, I think there are several reasons. We were piggybacking on the work of others at the start. One of the first things I did was contact Peter McNamara, because he had a magazine called *Aphelion* which lasted a few issues, and I'd become aware of Australian science fiction through that.

I also contacted the editor of *Far Out!*, a Western Australian-based magazine that lasted three issues, and said, 'Look, we want to start an Australian science fiction magazine. Can you tell us about the pitfalls? What should we do? What shouldn't we do?' They were both very generous with their comments and gave us great advice that saved early heartache.

So we did our research. Also, we were very ambitious. We thought, 'We're going to go big early. Let's not mess around.' We had a print run of 12,000 for each of the first two issues and we managed to get a deal with a big newsagency distributor. I didn't have a financial background, but I did look closely at how the finances would work from the start. The first few issues were very cheaply produced. I mean they were just stapled with block-colour covers, so we could do large volumes.

One of the key factors was that one of the partners in the venture was my brother, who's a printer. We needed to pay him of course, but we didn't have to pay him until we'd earnt some money from sales. We avoided the kind of thing that would have killed many print magazine back in those early days. So many of them folded after a few issues because in that first phase, when you're trying to build your sales, you're paying for issue after issue and the printing costs are mounting. We escaped that trap, so you might say we were fortunate to have a printer as a partner.

And how many of those 12,000 copies of the first issue did you sell?

With newsagency distribution, they'll tell you initially how many you've distributed, and then over a period of years, the copies that had been distributed trickle back as returns. So you actually don't get a final sales figure until quite a while after the event. I'd estimate we sold around 5000.

The way it worked initially was that Stephen Higgins and I both put in money to start the venture. That was back in 1990, and it was a fair investment for that time. We'd made our money back after those first couple of issues, plus a bit more, which helped us continue with the magazine.

Sales were reasonably good from the start. The idea of returns coming back from the newsagency was something I didn't really understand until it happened. We were expecting to sell something like 10,000 or so and it was a bit disappointing that we only reached 5000. We found out much later that these sorts of return figures were actually pretty good for a new magazine. It got us off to a fairly solid start. Then, because this was really wide coverage for a fiction magazine in Australia, we signed a lot of subscribers, which has been how we've survived since.

Not long after issue four, the distributor said to us, 'Look fellas, you're not really selling in the numbers you need for us to handle you.' These were the guys who handled magazines like *Cleo* and *Cosmopolitan*. They were the biggest distributor around and we were not in the right category for them. I'm still surprised they took us on in the first place. I think we approached them at a time when they were expanding. Anyway, their decision to drop us killed the mass-market idea for *Aurealis*.

We then made a deal with a smaller distributor who was less reliable.

We did okay for a few years but after that it became more difficult, and the numbers were nowhere near what we'd had in terms of sales. We became more reliant on subscribers after that.

You've said that if you'd known *Eidolon* was also planning to launch around the same time as *Aurealis*, you may have abandoned thoughts of starting the magazine. How do you view competition such as *Andromeda Spaceways*, or *Dimension6* now? Is there room for more publishers of short SF/F/H in Australia?

Back in 1990, when we published the first issue, there was no Australian science fiction and fantasy magazine and we were more motivated by the fact that we thought there *ought* to be. We knew it wasn't going to make huge amounts of money. *Aphelion* and *Far Out!* didn't survive financially. When we learned another magazine had started up at exactly the same time as *Aurealis*, we thought, 'This is going to be even more difficult financially than we had thought. If there's going to be an Australian science fiction and fantasy magazine anyway, do we need to be there as well?' Now, it's a completely different story. There's room for many more publications than there used to be because of the new publishing options.

As far as other Australian magazines go in the current landscape, I think they fill a different niche to *Aurealis*—their publishing philosophies are completely different. The mechanics of how they do things are different—I don't think there's any competition at all. We're all just trying to support Australian science fiction and fantasy.

If Harlan Ellison was right in 1998 when he said, 'Do you guys understand that this is the Golden Age of Australian science fiction?' What Age are we living in now?

In 1990, the first editorial we wrote was along the lines that Australia had never had a 'Golden Age' of science fiction, and that perhaps it was glimmering just up ahead. But at that particular time, things weren't looking too good. There was no magazine and no mainstream publisher was interested science fiction and fantasy in Australia, so we were trying to generate a bit of enthusiasm and hype around the idea. Often these sorts of declarations become self-fulfilling.

We heralded the Golden Age of Australian Science Fiction in that issue. Harlan Ellison, in the introduction to *Dreaming Down Under*, said, 'Do you guys know you're living in the Golden Age of Science Fiction?' I guess our response would be that not only did we know it, we were ones that declared it was just over the horizon ahead eight years before!

So if the Golden Age was back in the 1990s, what age are we in now?

I think we're still in the Golden Age!

Still in it?

Yeah, these Golden Ages can last quite a while. There are just so many Australian authors who've gone on to worldwide recognition from 1990 to now. The numbers have increased and things have constantly improved. We've played our part along the way, but there are so many other factors involved. I personally believe we are still in our Golden Age and it's becoming even more significant as time goes on.

Great news for writers and readers! So where does *Aurealis* sit on the world stage?

We've always said that we're an Australian magazine and we publish Australian, and to some degree New Zealand, authors. If we were to start opening up to absolutely everyone in the world then we're just another magazine like hundreds of others out there. Our point of difference is that we publish Australian writers.

At the beginning of 2016, however, we decided to introduce overseas authors into the mix. We made a decision that we wanted people outside of Australia to also read the magazine, but on the other hand, we didn't want to be just another magazine that had no point of distinction. We decided to maintain the number of stories we'd always published for Australian writers, and simply add one non-Australian story to each issue. We're continuing that this year, and the plan is to increase the readership without affecting the total number of works we publish from Australian writers.

David Farland, judge of *Writers of the Future* among other things, said recently that in his opinion Australian and English SF/F writers are generally more prepared to tackle deeper issues than their American counterparts. I think that describes the approach *Aurealis* takes. We publish pretty much anything that falls into the categories of science fiction, fantasy, and horror, and we allow writers to take their time a little bit to develop their stories. We're not solely action focused.

In terms of the world stage, there are a couple of strands to consider with Australian science fiction and fantasy. There's a strand which is indistinguishable from SF/F written anywhere else. It's written for a specific market and a lot of that is successful. In my view there's another strand which is a little more quirky and more experimental.

What are the biggest differences between *Aurealis* in September 1990, and *Aurealis* in May 2017?

In September 1990 the plan was for four print issues per year with eight to ten stories in each. We published two of these in 1990. The next year we managed four issues and it nearly killed us. We were so involved in producing the magazine, we had no time at all for marketing or promoting. Eventually we said, 'No, we can't keep doing this.' Then we wound it back to two issues a year. So for a long time it was two issues a year with five to ten stories in each, which meant ten to twenty stories a year.

Now we're publishing thirty stories a year and I think on average they're longer stories because space is not as much of an issue with digital publishing. So we're publishing more fiction. We're publishing more articles as well. We publish two articles an issue, or twenty a year, where we were only publishing two a year previously. We're also publishing many more book reviews than we ever did. So it's bigger. Bigger as well as better.

It's much easier to produce a digital magazine than a print magazine time-wise, but on the flipside, the stories have a shorter life which can be a little disappointing. It's not long before a given story is 'So last month!' and that's a shame. One of the criticisms we used to get was, 'You only come out twice a year. To be really successful you need to come out more regularly than that.'

That's one of the differences. We have a lot more time now to promote the magazine. I used to hate mailing out issues to subscribers. The process involved several days of people shoving magazines in envelopes. The conversion to digital was a big change for us and it's been extremely successful for all sorts of reasons. With print, the postage costs were continually increasing and we had to keep increasing our prices to match or we'd struggle financially. It was getting to the point where we thought, 'This isn't going to be viable anymore. We need to make a decision.' So we made the decision to go digital and haven't looked back.

Which leads nicely into my next question: Will we ever see *Aurealis* in print again?

We've made a foray back into print with *Aurealis #100*. Will this be a one-off? Who knows at this point? Every second publishing meeting we have, it comes up as an item for discussion. With print-on-demand we might be able to do something that's not going to break the bank. I would like to see it but the big problem with the viability of a magazine revolves around the workloads of the people involved. If we introduced print alongside our digital publications, workload would become an issue and I'm very wary of that. I mean it would be great to have a print issue as well but then everyone's got even more to do.

Over the years *Aurealis* has published early works by some of this country's best-known SF and fantasy writers, including the likes of KJ Bishop, Simon Brown, Stephen Dedman, Shane Dix, Kaaron Warren, Sean Williams, Trudi Canavan, and more recently Thoraiya Dyer. What does it mean to you to have played a part in supporting Australian SF and fantasy writers?

Supporting these guys really is the most satisfying part of the job. It's fantastic to unearth new talent. And the number of people we've published and then seen go on to great things is just amazing. Trudi was our art director. She was in charge of commissioning the artwork and she used to lay out the magazine. She was important to us for a long stretch.

Look at Shaun Tan. He went on to win an academy award, and the world's biggest children's book award. It's pretty amazing when you think of all the people who've got their start with *Aurealis*. So many of these guys have gone on to bigger and better things, and we just love the fact that we're able to play a part in that process in people's careers. It's terrific.

You're also a founder of the Aurealis Awards, which are arguably more famous than the magazine. What was the original purpose of the Awards?

Well firstly, the Awards aren't *arguably* more famous than the magazine, they are *definitely* more famous, which is interesting because they were an offshoot of the magazine in a sense. When we started *Aurealis*, Stephen Higgins, Peter MacNamara and a few others tried to start an award. We already had the Ditmars, but there was no peer-assessed award. There was no equivalent of the World Fantasy Award.

That initial push for an award failed because everyone had a different idea of how it should work, and the discussion just went around in circles. A few years later I thought, 'As a magazine we're in a position to have a go at this. We're well known enough now that we may be able to set something up.'

At that time I came up with what I felt was a good structure for an award. I thought, 'What's the worst that can happen here? Maybe we declare some winners and no-one is interested. So what? No-one can stop us saying what *Aurealis* considers to be the best SF novel for a particular year.'

I contacted a number of people in fandom and in the industry and asked them if they wanted to be a judge and gave them the guidelines and timeframes I'd come up with. At first there wasn't a structured submission process because we felt very few people would submit to an award they'd never heard of. We didn't want the Awards to consider only those works that had been submitted. It was up to the judges to hunt down all the eligible books and pass them on to each other. This wasn't quite as onerous as it sounds in the early years because back then there weren't as many qualifying works as now, and often the judges were keen to read them anyway.

It was like that at first. We had no money then, so at the very first Awards night we gave out certificates instead of trophies. We advertised the night and quite a few people came. It made a bit of a splash and the whole thing snowballed from there. The Awards have always run on volunteers. They were always a cost in time and money to the magazine, so it came to a point where, as a group, we couldn't manage both the magazine and the Awards as they grew. We had to outsource the Awards and find alternative groups to run them. Lots of people have been involved with the Awards over the years and it's gone from strength to strength.

At the start I insisted that the judges sign a statement indicating they'd read all the books in a category, which to me is the absolute base-level requirement for being a judge on these sorts of awards. It seemed a straightforward proposition. You have intelligent readers, people who've read widely in the genre, reading all the books in a category, then deciding which are the best, and arguing it out amongst themselves. I personally haven't agreed with every decision. You can always put forward counterarguments, but the process is pretty good and it's stood the test of time.

You can't please everyone. There are always those who'll want to complain but if the basic structure is good everything should work out okay in the long run.

Where to from here for *Aurealis* magazine?

I personally see something involving print potentially coming on in tandem with our digital magazine. We've previously been print only, or digital only. We haven't done both before, so *Aurealis #100* is a first in many ways.

A few years back we totally overhauled our website, and the improvements we put in place there included structural things like making it easier to subscribe as well as giving it a stunning look from a design perspective. From a fiction point of view, our big change was to add an overseas story to each issue. We're waiting to see how that goes before planning the next evolution of *Aurealis*. Sometimes you have to wait until the next idea hits you, and that idea only becomes obvious in retrospect. But whatever the next change is, it's always the fiction that defines us.

I'd like to see *Aurealis* continue to increase its profile and become a magazine which features in the consciousness of readers and fandom worldwide.

The Author: Chris Large

Chris is an Australian writer of science fiction and fantasy. His work has appeared in *Aurealis* and *Andromeda Spaceways Magazine*, and in anthologies published by Ticonderoga Publications, Dark Prints Press and CSFG Publishing. He has received mentions in Ellen Datlow's Best Horror of the Year series, and Year's Best YA Speculative Fiction from Twelfth Planet Press.

Secret History of Australia
Archibald Cistoon (1810–1888)
Researched by Michael Pryor

One of Australia's greatest all round athletes, Archibald Cistoon's prowess was discovered at an early age when he began to walk at only two months of age. At the age of five months he was able to pin his mother two falls out of three, and by his first birthday he showed that he could bowl a wicked in-swinger.

Raised in Goulburn (NSW), Archibald Cistoon was recognised for his athletic feats throughout country NSW. In his teens he completed astounding feats of speed, strength and endurance. In 1825 he and his horse Big Boy cleared a fence eight feet high. Then the young Archibald Cistoon repeated the feat, swapping places with the horse and carrying it while leaping over the barrier. In 1826 he wheeled a wheelbarrow full of bricks for twenty-four hours non-stop, ending up a hundred miles from Goulburn. He built a neat one-room cottage from the bricks before running home backwards all the way, arriving only ten hours later.

Archibald Cistoon eschewed team sports, preferring to test his solo mettle. Therefore, he excelled in wood chopping, pig wrestling, freeform ice sculpture and modelling, while also setting a number of records on the billiards table where his 'Thunderbolt' cannon was renowned for the force with which he struck the white, leaving many spectators temporarily deafened.

By the age of twenty, Archibald Cistoon was tired of conventional sporting exploits and turned his hand to increasingly bizarre tests of his ability. In 1831 he ran from Goulburn to Sydney and back dressed as the Mad Hatter from *Alice in Wonderland*. In 1832 he carried a pig on his back while he completed 10,000 one-handed push-ups in a single day. In 1833 he towed a steam locomotive by his teeth while painting a portrait of the Governor.

After many more increasingly strange efforts, Archibald Cistoon joined the circus as a combination strong man and lion tamer, but was dismissed after wrestling two lions and a tiger in a display that left all three big cats traumatised. Shamed and guilty, Archibald Cistoon stowed away on a ship bound for New Zealand but drowned in a freak accident while drunk, wrapped up in iron chains and locked inside a steamer trunk.

Reviews

Corpselight
Verity Fassbinder book 2
Angela Slatter
Jo Fletcher Books
Review by Aimée Lindorff

Verity Fassbinder returns in Angela Slatter's latest work *Corpselight*, successor to her wildly popular (at least to the *Aurealis* team) debut, *Vigil*.

Still recovering from the events of *Vigil*, and surrounded by increasingly *un*-fun tasks of pending motherhood, Verity finds herself running the less perilous end of investigations—insurance. A claim of 'Unusual Happenstance' sets her sights on Walsh & Penhalligon, while dry-land drownings put her new family in the path of danger. Add to the mix mysterious kitsune assassins and the return of a long-lost relative, and maternity leave is proving more and more dangerous in Weyrd Brisbane.

The challenge of any second book in a series is to not only capture the spirit and tone of the first but also expand on the world established. Slatter's skills in mosaic short story world-building are ably employed here, painting a rich foundation of mythology, character, and setting that leaves you forever wanting more from Brisneyland. Drawn among the untapped setting of Brisbane, the true delight for this reader is the familiarity of place in *Corpselight* and its predecessor *Vigil*. Brisbane is wrought live on the page through vivid prose and meaningful detail, and it's refreshing and comforting to experience a speculative tale in your own backyard (almost literally). West End cafés play host to magical regulars and the tangle of trees in New Farm Park hides thievish sprites.

Verity Fassbinder is just as vibrant, capable of walking off the page at any second. Disgruntled at her situation, but perpetually curious and fiercely loyal, Fassbinder could well be one of the best Australian speculative characters of any era. Slatter's gift for dialogue beautifully renders her cast. From supportive Normal partner David to the ever-mysterious Misses Norn, perpetually disgruntled police liaison Rhonda to protector, *jäger*, and friend Ziggi, Slatter paints a cast of unforgettable characters, each embodied in true affection and magic.

If you haven't already met Verity Fassbinder and crew, then you are sorely missing out on the year's best Australian supernatural noir.

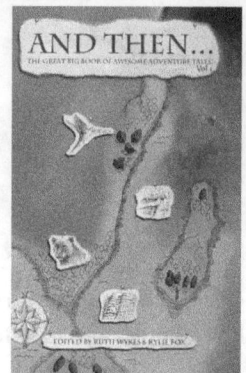

And Then...
The Great Big Book of Awesome Adventure Tales
Volume 1.
Edited by Kylie Fox and Ruth Wykes
Clan Destine Press
Review by Deanne Sheldon-Collins

And Then is, as its title promises, a great big book. The anthology contains 15 tales, a mix of novellas and short stories, and there are more to come in Volume 2. The collection is a genre mash-up that spans sci-fi, fantasy, historical fiction, crime, and romance—but, first and foremost, these are tales of adventure.

And Then began with a callout to Australian authors, for adventure stories with two protagonists. Such criteria suggest a mix of action and characterisation—two elements often seen as mutually exclusive—and the resulting anthology delivers on this promise.

Particularly notable is Jason Franks's 'Exli and the Dragon', in which two thieves—one human, one an advanced lifeform shaped like a pillow—team up to escape an asteroid prison. Told from the not-a-pillow's perspective, the story is full of clinical yet endearing observations about how humans appear from the outside, insights both hilarious and thought-provoking.

Another standout story is 'Death at the Dragon Circus' by Tansy Rayner Roberts, in which two assassins join the circus while starting a new life together. A brood of baby dragons enlivens the already vibrant circus backdrop, but the real heart of the story is the assassins' profound relationship and their search for new selves.

Many of the tales feel like glimpses of longer stories. This is common in speculative short fiction, since epic premises and detailed world-building don't lend themselves well to brief, one-off stories. This doesn't detract from the collection, however; instead, it whets the reader's appetite for more.

And Then traipses across galaxies, countries, and time periods, but it has a distinctly Australian flavour. Well-known authors include Sophie Masson, Alan Baxter, and Lucy Sussex. Stories take place in Gold Rush Ballarat, contemporary Brisbane and Melbourne, near-future Sydney. Circus dragons snack on banksia cones and breathe eucalyptus-scented smoke. *And Then* is a fun, varied read—swashbuckling genre fiction with an antipodean atmosphere.

The Wizardry of Jewish Women

Gillian Polack
Satalyte Publishing
Review by Rebecca McEwen

One of Gillian Polack's great strengths is finding the magical in the mundane and the mundane in the magical. Although *The Wizardry of Jewish Women* is a story about magic, it is also a story about family, the many different forms of love, secrecy, gender, identity, and politics.

When sisters Belinda and Judith receive a box of their great-grandmother's possessions, including a very unusual scrapbook, they find themselves drawn into the secrets of their heritage. Meanwhile, Rhonda, a historian and fan-fiction author with prophetic abilities, tries to keep her talents a secret from both those who know her personally and those in the online communities that are both a refuge and a threat to her anonymity.

Polack's sparse prose and the shifts between the characters and the first and third person knock the reader off balance, providing both the momentum of the story and the connection between seemingly disparate elements. Interspersed with wry moments of humour (along with a laughing lemon tree and a hidden unicorn), Polack's narrative weaves magic into the everyday lives of the protagonists with unusual pragmatism. Some of the online dialogue—extracts from Rhonda's chats and memes—may not sit well with all readers, given the range of online language and experiences, but that is the only jarring note in the otherwise flowing prose.

'[W]omen's stuff is supposed to be petty and small and inconsequential,' observes one of the characters, '[e]ven when it's the whole world.' The delicate exploration of the protagonists, their relationships, and their lives leaves much unsaid, but it never denies the complexity of the women, the heart of the story, and the gravity of their experiences.

This review is of the first edition of *Wizardry*, published by Satalyte. A new edition and publisher will be announced soon.

The Djinn Falls in Love and Other Stories
Edited by Mahvesh Murad and Jared Shurin
Solaris
Review by Chris Foster

A magic lamp woven from page and ink, waiting for readers to release the djinn.

Originally titled *Djinnthology* to cover the broad range of djinn (also known as 'jinn' or, more famously, 'genie' in Disney's *Aladdin*), it is the Egyptian poet Hermes's piece that the book was ultimately named after. Do not be fooled, however, as the 21 short stories within are as deceptive and different as the djinn they describe. This collection is aimed at adults, not children, filled with graphic tales of trickery, displacement, belonging (or lack of), power, greed, lust, and love.

Right from the inception of this collection, the editors wanted to handle the topic with care and compassion. The djinn have many different interpretations in different cultures, something the editors respected by keeping local spelling for each story. This allows the authors to be authentic in their prose, while taking the reader through the beliefs of different regions of our world unbiased by editorial formalities. More than anything, it makes the writing feel *real*. These are the streets we walk.

The authors are from across the globe, masters of their craft ranging from Saad Z Hossain to Sami Shah to Claire North. There is no pulling back, each tale raw like the world we live in. Murder, loneliness, the frailty of life, and the urge to belong are just some of the themes. The entire book collapses the idea that djinn are magical beings of great mystery, instead portraying them as very human. Where would you live if suddenly you were drawn into our world? What if your power for wishes was gone—what would you have left? It is this mature handling (along with plenty of twists, turns, and consequences) that makes *The Djinn Falls in Love and Other Stories* such a compelling read. It is not the djinn but ourselves we learn most about.

An illuminating, smokeless light into our world and the djinn who live among us. Easily a book one could fall in love with.

The Transmigration of Bodies
and
Signs Preceding the End of the World
Yuri Herrera
Text Publishing
Review by Stephanie McLeay

These two novellas are a testament to the fine work that can come from a magnificent writer paired with a talented translator. The themes are heavy. *The Transmigration of Bodies* explores the rot inside a society, as the Redeemer sets about trying to find the meaning behind a newly sparked feud. *Signs Preceding the End of the World* takes you on a Dante-like journey as Makina 'verses' to find her brother, not knowing she can never go back. The journeys of both protagonists are felt even more deeply for how skilfully Yuri Herrera wraps you in the skin of their worlds.

Only a few sentences in, and it's evident that the essence of Herrera's style has been captured; the writing is idiomatic and foreign, and yet has a familiar feel of the intimately colloquial. In a few sparsely punctuated words, littered with idioms and carefully untranslated terms, Herrera entangles you in the bodies of first the Redeemer, and then Makina.

'Feel' is the correct word for the writing. The sparse, bleak descriptions, reminiscent of Cormac McCarthy's *The Road*, do not conjure a vivid mental image but they do capture an incredible sensory landscape. In *The Transmigration of Bodies*, the oppressive, fetid, claustrophobic emptiness of the hastily abandoned streets the Redeemer drives through can be felt close around you. All this is more in impressions than descriptions. The chilling effect of a short, haunting moment is solidified by a simple sentence: 'The scene had the innocence of all unsettling things that take place in silence.'

This book will grip onto you tightly as you read, and stay with you long after you've finished.

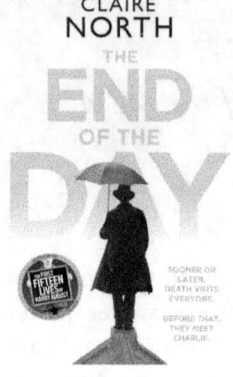

The End of the Day
Claire North
Hachette Australia
Review by Robert Goodman

It is a brave author who will take on the personification of Death after Terry Pratchett. Claire North almost sidesteps the issue by instead focusing on the Harbinger of Death, the one who goes before as a courtesy or warning, currently an ordinary Englishman called Charlie.

Charlie is a bit of a cipher. A non-threatening everyman who seems able to relate to (and communicate with) practically everyone he meets, who tends to look at the bright side of life (and death). It seems limiting for Death to only have one human harbinger in a world of seven billion people but, while there is a back office to support him, there is no suggestion that Charlie is part of a bigger team of harbingers fanning out around the world.

As with North's earlier novels, *The End of the Day* is a bit of a travelogue. Charlie finds himself in Greenland, Mexico, Russia, Syria, and Nigeria, to name a few. He is sent to these places carrying meaningful gifts for those he visits. Not all of those people die. Some of them can take the visit and the message behind the gift as a warning and change their lives. And not all visits are about the end of a life; in North's world, Death also comes to witness the end of an idea or an era.

But this is also a bit of an issue-logue. There is little in the way of plot, as the novel is essentially a series of vignettes, bookended with pointed anonymous conversation snippets that cover a shopping list of causes. These include climate change, rampant development, nationalism, populism, same-sex relationships, religious tolerance, sectarian wars. It is absolutely valid for novels to deal with current social issues. But this heavy-handed approach, over such a wide range of issues, wears very quickly.

There is plenty to think about in *The End of the Day*. When Death is one of your main characters, questions about life and its meaning are going to work their way into the plot. But in the end, these deeper questions, and the book as a whole, are weighed down by the sheer number of issues that North has tried to tackle.

www.ingramcontent.com/pod-product-compliance
Lightning Source LLC
Chambersburg PA
CBHW051345020726
47501CB00007B/2277